Immortal Obsession

A NOVEL

DENISE K. RAGO

ISBN: 145287753X

ISBN-13: 9781452877532

Library of Congress Control Number: 2010907232

DEDICATION

For Marvin

Tracy,

I hope you enjoy.
immortal obsession
and the world of my
vampires.

Thank you!

Enjoy —

Denise K. Rago

Prologue - Paris 1790

❦

THICK, BILLOWING SMOKE filled the Louis XVI apartment as flames climbed the brocade drapes, spreading from the valance to the ceiling. Christian Du Mauré felt the eyes of his best friend, Michel Baptiste, on him from the doorway, as Christian hung on to his mortal lover, Josette Delacore. Christian had dreaded the inevitability of this moment since the night they had met when he had seen her walking along the Pont Neuf on the arm of the salacious vampire, Gaétan. Rumors had escalated about his new mortal mistress and there she was by his side, a dark beauty with a warm smile and a lilting laugh. Christian had not planned to fall in love with her, but that had been three years ago, and so much had changed in such a short time. Here they stood in her bedroom trying to say good-bye.

"We must go, Josette," he yelled over the roaring fire, gesturing to Michel. He knew it was time, yet he hesitated, holding her tighter, feeling her sweat through her pale blue gown. She had grown thinner. He guessed she was not eating. Although they never spoke of it, they both knew the Delacores' arrest and execution were imminent.

"I know." Her muffled cries made his heart ache. "Despite what happens, I will always love you Christian. I could not convince Luc to leave here—"

He silenced her with another kiss. She was trembling, fighting hysteria as he held her tighter. He swallowed his own grief at the thought of never seeing her again, never making love to her right under her husband's nose in this very bedroom. Soon it would all be ashes, and their love affair just a memory. The past few years now felt like moments.

"I have something you must take with you." She pulled away from him, frantically searching under the mattress. He studied her angular face, surrounded by wavy brown hair falling to her shoulders. It was hard to imagine never seeing her again.

"I gave her valise to the Meraux's already."

She continued groping under the mattress. "There's just one more thing."

"Josette, we must be on that ship by dawn," he begged, watching the flames curl across the ceiling. He and Michel could survive accidents that would kill a mortal, such as Josette, but fire meant death to any vampire.

"Here, take this." She handed him a small leather box that he recognized. "It's all I have, but you will need it to pay for Solange's care."

Her emerald eyes looked past him at Michel who stood beside him now and for a moment she felt like a stranger. Christian was sure that something had just passed between his best friend and his lover but pride and time kept him from asking.

"Mon ami," Michel whispered. "Hurry, before there is no way out for any of us." He tugged on his best friend's lace cuff, grievously watching the two of them.

"These were presents to you, my love." Christian sighed, fighting back tears. It seemed only fitting that he should take her jewelry; the last vestige of their love affair as the reality of their parting covered him like a blanket.

"I have no more use for them. You, Michel, and Solange need them now. Hurry before you can't get out. "

She had always been so strong. Rejecting Gaétan and coming to his bed had been an unimaginable act of defiance. The older, more powerful vampire had laughed it off, trying to hide his embarrassment at losing her to a younger rival, but Christian knew the cost of loving her. The growing disdain between the two vampires had become a bitter rivalry. Even Gabrielle, his lover and maker, resented losing his attention to a mortal aristocrat and would not protect him from the vengeful Gaétan. The Parisian vampires had become even further divided, mirroring the mortal world, and so it was time to leave Paris.

"Christian, we must go now." Michel watched the flames spread across the wooden floor coming toward them.

Christian ignored him, though kissing Josette and holding her close seemed meaningless now, empty gestures for ineffable feelings. He looked once more at his mortal lover, framed against the luxurious bedroom they had shared, and tried to imagine his life without her, a time in the future when this would be a distant memory with no feelings attached to it. Perhaps that was the only way to survive the here and now.

"Solange?" She whispered, pulling at his arm. She tangled her fingers in a strand of his flowing blond hair and stared into his dark eyes. "I told Luc—"

"She's already in London." He smiled. "You have nothing to worry about, ever."

"M'lady," Michel whispered, brushing a strand of hair from her face. "Good-bye."

Christian fought acknowledging the tenderness between them.

"Michel." His name left her lips as if it pained her to say it aloud, and their eyes locked for the second time.

"Thank you for loving me," Christian whispered, pulling her close for the last time. Her hair smelled like roses underneath all the smoke. He ran his hands through it, trying to savor the moment. He fought to release her, and then they were gone. He followed Michel out of her apartment and down into the streets of Paris as black smoke poured from the windows. The shrill of the crowd was deafening, and they found themselves face-to-face with an oncoming mob. Christian heard Michel curse as they ducked into the shadows of the Quai du Louvre and headed toward an alley that would lead them to a dirt path along the Seine. The air smelled of sweat, ashes, and blood.

"We must be on the *Cométe* by dawn," Michel yelled, barely able to breathe through all the smoke. "I told François to meet us near the Pont Royal at midnight. Come on."

Michel grabbed Christian's hand, and the two friends moved through the shadows of the royal palace toward the Pont Neuf. The sounds and scents of all the bodies, blood, and flesh tickled their hunger, awakening the urge to feed again.

"Get us out of this crowd," Christian murmured, holding the leather box to his chest as throngs of men yelling and carrying torches marched past them. Suppose François was not waiting for them. Suppose he had been attacked by the mob? The catacombs were no longer a safe haven. *Perhaps a mausoleum at dawn,* he thought as they sidled up against the cold stone of the royal palace waiting for the carriage to arrive on the Pont Neuf.

Michel spotted it and quickly the two vampires skirted the crowd and slid into the shoddy carriage. François cursed the crowds as they wound their way down to meet the launch that would take them out to their ship. The carriage plowed through the narrow streets, the wheels splashing mud on pedestrians as they rambled toward the quay.

Michel paid up as they scampered onto the launch. Christian kept his eyes on the water, never looking back at his beautiful city as the smoke and flames became tiny spots in the distance. Michel sang songs into the darkness, as they rowed over whitecaps and the sea breeze hit their faces. Christian spotted the *Cométe* and felt himself relax, anticipating a new life for them both.

"I cannot believe I paid for this hovel!" Michel collapsed his 6'4" frame onto the straw-covered wooden bunk.

The vampires could barely stand in the narrow, dank room, complete with a steamer trunk, a mirror nailed to the wall, and a chamber pot rolling around in the corner. The smell of soot from their clothes added to the odor of urine and rotting wood permeating the air. Christian ignored Michel and sat on the floor. The rocking ship soothed him. He reached for the lantern and put it on the floor beside him. Hesitantly, he opened Josette's jewelry box. A piece of paper slipped out and caught in the moonlight. He pulled the lantern closer to read the note.

16 July 1790

Christian,

By the time you read this note, I pray you and Michel will have made it safely to England, far away from this horrible place. I shall miss France. My only regret is not having more time with you, my love. As I face my certain death there is something I must tell you. Being the lover of not one but two vampires spoiled me forever, and once I entered your world, I could no longer share my mortal husband's bed. Luc is not Solange's father as I have always led him to believe. You are. Please understand that I never wanted to burden you or make you feel you were responsible for her. You often spoke of your regrets at not being a husband and a father and I yearned to tell you. Much has changed, Christian. She is your daughter. I know you will find a good home for her, but please watch over her and know that I will love you forever.

Josette

Christian glanced at Michel, who was curled up asleep like a cat. He impulsively reached over to wake him and thought better of it. Rereading the note again, a bloody tear ran down his cheek. Paris and his young lover were gone, victims of a disease that had turned brother against brother, and Place de Grève into a bloody nightmare. Mortals called it La Révolution Française, but he saw no sense in it.

Shaking his head, he reread the note once more in disbelief. He had sired a child with a mortal woman. Did the Parisian vampires know of Solange's parentage? Would Gabrielle kill his hybrid child, or consider her a threat to the pure vampire blood that coursed through their veins? Would she be safe in London? After all, their destination was no secret. Christian vowed to watch over his daughter from a distance as she navigated the mortal world; protect her from his kind, yet not interfere in her life.

As more tears fell, Christian folded the note and tucked it back into the jewelry box. He felt the rays of the sun as the need to sleep overcame him. Sliding next to Michel, he drifted into oblivion, just as he had every morning for the past thirty-three years, unable to fight the dawn's deathlike embrace. How Michel would laugh at him when he told him he had fathered a child with Josette. Clutching the box to his chest, his last conscious thought turned to Solange, his mortal daughter. *At least she is safe.*

PART ONE
NEW YORK—PRESENT DAY

Chapter One

THE VAMPIRE CLOSED his eyes and bit into the fleshy neck of the waif. He waited for the rush as the red plasma trickled down his throat, engorging him and bringing him to life. He heard the young man moaning in ecstasy, his voice echoing through him, drowning out the loud club music surrounding them both. Blood flowed through his body like fire as Lucien instinctively wrapped the trembling stray tighter in his strong arms. The boy's muscles tightened, his heart beating faster. He was afraid. Lucien felt stronger as the urchin's blood coursed through his veins, inflating him, making him dizzy with power.

Strangely, he felt mortal again; his sight became even clearer and the surrounding sounds intensified, almost to the point of pain. The youth's heartbeat pounded in his ears like native drums, and between his legs an erection bulged as blood filled every inch of his body. For a moment Lucien thought he might die. Not like his mortal death, but in bliss like a star, blazing so bright he would explode, shattering the dark universe with fragments of energy and light.

The blood gave him incredible sustenance and power. It pulled at his own thoughts seductively and slowly, like a vampire tugging at his victim's life force. It felt as if the blood had a life of its own, a vampiric power. Lucien concentrated harder as images from the young man's life ran through his own body: a tiny house, his bedroom, school, friends, putting a needle in his veins. The images moved like a film in fast forward. The face of a dark-haired woman with emerald eyes surfaced. Once a child, now a seductively beautiful woman. Was she a lover? No.

A sister, perhaps? She reminded him of someone he had known in Paris, but who? Reluctantly, Lucien released himself from the youthful flesh of his prey, still holding him close. The boy stared up at him with glazed eyes.

So the rumors had been true.

"Why'd you stop?" The boy rubbed his neck, feeling the two raised bumps.

"Too much of a good thing." Lucien smiled and licked his pouty lips. He brushed the mortal's warm cheek. Yes, if he were not careful, he would drain the boy. Instead, he studied him carefully, now that he had satisfied his lust for blood. He brushed a strand of dirty dark hair from the boy's sunken face. He was beautiful underneath his drug-induced haze.

"I'll do whatever you want as long as you pay me."

Lucien reached into the pocket of his leather coat for the wad of cash and felt nothing.

"Later I can get you all the money you could want, young man."

"It's Ryan," he quipped, his eyes glazed over from the blood loss. "I'm always available."

"Very well, Ryan. Who is the woman with the emerald eyes?"

"My sister Amanda." He chuckled nervously, knowing a vampire could gather information from a mortal's blood.

"She's beautiful."

"Yeah, and real smart. She got it all, beauty and brains."

Lucien had seen the facade of a large building with columns and banners waving in the breeze. He had seen a fountain with a beautiful angel on top, while running water and sunlight cascaded under her feet. The dark haired woman sat at a desk in a tiny office, surrounded by books and coffee cups, staring at a computer screen.

"She works in a museum." Ryan volunteered. "She loves antiques and anything French."

"Good taste." Lucien smiled as he caught a glimpse of Michel moving through the crowd coming toward them.

"Later, Ryan," he whispered in a dismissive tone.

Ryan nodded and ducked into the shadows. Lucien guessed this was the usual crowd of mostly young women, overly made up, dressed all in black, pretending to be one of the undead. Only in America, he thought, feeling suddenly homesick for the City of Lights. This was his first weekend in the New World, and already he missed Paris.

He watched Michel move through the crowd. Despite the passing centuries, Lucien had never forgotten Michel's grace and beauty, now adorned in haute couture such as Armani and Versace. Well over six feet tall, with catlike dark eyes, shoulder-length black hair, and high cheekbones, Michel was still one of the most beautiful men he had ever seen. He had been the talk of Paris centuries ago, and judging by the way women stared at him, Lucien assumed nothing had changed for the ethereal vampire. His beauty was arresting, his attraction to both sexes universal. He moved like a tiger through jungle palms, silent and deadly. Lucien felt his heart racing as Michel approached him.

"I thought it was just talk, but no." Michel gave Lucien the once-over. He had never trusted the younger vampire. "What brings you to our little corner of the world?"

"Quelling rumors." Lucien smiled carefully. There was no use lying.

"And how are our Parisian friends, Lucien?" Michel leaned up against the bar, scanning the crowd for Christian. Lucien's presence was an omen. "What are their panties in a bunch about now?" He grabbed a plastic drink straw from the bar and began to chew on it.

Lucien shrugged. He had come to New York to gather information. He had not asked for permission, nor would it have been granted to him. He was depending on the reputed good manners of the New York vampires, especially Christian Du Mauré, Michel's best friend. In fact, he was praying for it.

"I mean no harm, Michel." Lucien put his hands up in a gesture of humbleness. "It has been too long since we have seen each other." He noticed that Michel had only a trace of the French accent that Lucien remembered mixed with what must be a New York twang. He had heard that Christian and Michel had been here since the early 1900s.

"1790 to be exact." Michel spoke, twirling the straw. "If I remember correctly, you sided with Gaétan and Gabrielle against us, but then, that was over two hundred years ago. My memory may be failing." He watched Lucien carefully, guessing that he wanted no trouble, at least not in public.

"Things change, Michel. That is one of the advantages to being immortal. Your perspective on history alters at some point, don't you think?"

"Vampires tend to hold grudges. You should know that, Lucien."

Lucien shrugged, leaning against the bar.

"Well, my eyes deceive me." A deep, soothing voice pierced the darkness.

Lucien turned and found himself face-to-face with the flowing blond hair and dark eyes that could only belong to one immortal: Christian Du Mauré. Dressed in satin trousers and a lace shirt, he could almost pass for the eighteenth-century dandy Lucien remembered so well. He wore a long black leather overcoat and his once shoulder-length hair now fell down his back.

"Hello, Christian."

"Welcome to New York." Christian tried to smile, though it pained him. "What brings you to the Grey Wolf?" It took all of his self-control not to lunge at his enemy. Unfortunately, there were too many mortals present to draw that kind of attention.

"It has been too long since I saw my old friends."

"You were always a pitiful liar, Lucien." Christian instinctively touched the leather strap on his chest that held a machete strapped against his back, under his leather duster.

"What has happened to that well known politesse?" Lucien smiled, remembering there was no charming Christian.

"You come here without permission. If my memory serves me, that is an open declaration of war. I suggest that you leave before I lose my patience and you lose your head."

Christian had taken to wearing the machete since the nightmares had returned; faceless ghouls stalking him in Central Park. Lucien knew he would have been dead if not for the watchful eyes of the mortals around them, and he used it to his advantage. Christian knew he was here for a reason, and feared it.

The tall vampire kept an eye on Lucien who watched Ryan move through the crowd toward the door. *Has he fed from him yet?* Christian wondered, knowing that it would only be a matter of time. Then he could go back to Paris and squeal like a stuck pig.

"Kindness is a luxury in short supply these days. Now get out," Christian hissed. "Do not come back, or I will kill you."

Lucien forced a smile and stepped into the crowd of mortals as he made his way toward the exit. Once outside the club, the vampire reached for his cell phone as he followed young Ryan Perretti down Bleeker Street.

Chapter Two

"Do you think—" Michel paused, glancing around the club.

"Even if Gaétan were here, we wouldn't know it until he oozed out of the shadows like puss from a wound. Lucien is *her* soldier, Michel."

Christian dared not say her name, as if to do so would cause the pitiless bloodsucker to materialize before them. He tried not to think about Solange, but something was coming from across the sea. He felt it in his bones, but he tried not to give it a name or a face.

"Would you consider contacting Gabrielle?" Michel asked nonchalantly, twisting the straw around in his mouth as he eyed a young redhead at the bar.

"You know the answer to that one, my friend." Christian brushed Michel's cheek, holding his dark gaze. "You forget how we left her. She has a very long memory and would rather die than aid us now."

"I disagree. A woman scorned, definitely; in love with you, forever. You plan on following him?" Michel gestured toward the door.

"Need you ask?" Christian scowled. "I'll be back. Call me if any other uninvited guests show up."

Christian left the Grey Wolf and strolled down Bleeker Street. He followed Lucien's scent toward Seventh Avenue. The vampire was on foot, most likely following someone. *Is he following Ryan?* Christian sensed that Lucien had not come to New York alone. *Who would have come with him?* He kept a safe distance, turning left onto Seventh Avenue and heading uptown toward Time Square. They were always present, haunting his thoughts. The ruling class of French vampires he had known in Paris prior to La Révolution Française. Made up of Gaétan, Gabrielle, Lucien, Étienne, and Antoine, plus a host of less powerful bloodsuckers, they had once all mingled with the minor aristocracy, taking them as their mortal lovers.

Then La Révolution Française had come and the Parisian vampires had turned against one another in a bid for control, igniting their own civil war. Like their human counterparts, they chose sides and slaughtered one another. Christian remembered how Gabrielle had enjoyed indiscriminately seducing and slaughtering the young vampires she took to her bed. She relished drinking their blood, just as the New Regime gorged themselves on the aged champagne of the French aristocrats; and he despised her for it. As her influence grew, she took a new lover, an older, more powerful vampire named Gaétan. Their union ignited more unrest amongst the vampires.

The bright lights of Times Square illuminated his white skin and cascading hair. Christian dodged the crowds, following Lucien's scent across Broadway and up Seventh Avenue, careful to stay downwind of him. The scent of another immortal filled his senses, coming from the east. *Definitely an outsider, but who this time?*

His thoughts turned again to Gabrielle and he shivered inside. The machete on his back gave him comfort as he wove his way through the frenetic mortals, scurrying about like ants on such a cool summer night. The streets were congested and noisy, distracting him as he followed the scent of the two vampires heading north. *Damn lackeys.*

Christian had always hated politics, and though he managed to elude the wars of mortals, he could not escape the petty jealousies of his own kind. He found his own kind more vengeful and cruel than human beings. Perhaps having eternity to let wounds fester gave them an edge. He had always been a loner, bowing to no one, not even the vampiress who had made him.

Gabrielle and Gaétan lived by their own arbitrary rules, slaughtering those who would not swear their loyalty to them. She had taken both his and Michel's loyalty for granted. Christian reflected on that infamous night the vampires had met in the catacombs, asking permission to leave her and Paris forever. They knew how vain and full of pride and greed Gabrielle was. She would never acquiesce. Despite her anger toward him, she wished to keep both of them by her side forever.

The vampires hid in the catacombs as the city burned above them. They had asked and she had said no. Forever short on patience, Michel began to argue with her and Gaétan stepped into the fight. In the glow of the torchlight, Christian saw Michel pull a dagger from his coat. Christian charged him before he could reach Gabrielle, knowing he would plunge the dagger into her heart, but not before

Gaétan came between them, trying to protect her as well. In one quick movement, Michel pinned Gaétan to his chest with the dagger against his heart.

"Michel, no!" Gabrielle's high-pitched scream bounced off the dirt ceiling. Her beautiful face was a kaleidoscope of rage, panic, and fear.

"I told you, we are leaving here tonight. Now, shall I cut out his pathetic heart, or do you let us leave?" Michel held Gaétan tight as he struggled. He ripped open Gaétan's black shirt and plunged the knife into his chest. Blood gushed down to his navel.

"Let him go, Michel," she hissed, stopping as if she had hit a wall. "Your defiance will not be tolerated." Michel continued to push the knife into the vampire's chest as his screams echoed throughout the catacombs.

"When did you turn against us?" She snarled, though Christian could hear the fear in her voice. Michel had always been unpredictable; the thing Gabrielle loved yet feared the most about him.

"When you began slaughtering our kind," Michel hissed, struggling to hold Gaétan as he pushed the knife in deeper.

"Please, Michel, spare him." Gabrielle begged. "You can go, just release him."

Michel loosened his grip on the weak vampire and pulled the dagger out of his chest.

"I'll slaughter you," Gaétan stuttered, his brown eyes ablaze with anger.

"You are going to do what?" Michel yelled, plunging the dagger back into his chest again. Blood spurted onto Michel's hand, turning the dagger a deep red. Both Gaétan and Gabrielle screamed as Michel twisted the dagger.

"Perhaps I should cut your heart out and eat it in front of you," he whispered into the vampire's ear.

"You will kill him, Michel, please," Gabrielle screamed. "Christian, make him listen to reason."

Michel pushed the bloodsucker onto his knees and then sliced his own arm, forcing Gabrielle's second in command to drink from his thin wrist while none of the other vampires moved to intercede. Christian thought it one of Michel's bravest moments, but as usual, Michel had taken things too far.

Pulling Gaétan up from the dirt floor and pinning both arms behind him, Michel had invited Christian to drink from his enemy. Christian had buried his face in Gaétan's gaping wound and taken his life force. Christian had wanted to kill him but stopped himself after having gotten what they had come for, safe passage out of France. Christian remembered feeling powerful as he licked the warm blood off his nemesis's lips and stared into the dark eyes of his adversary.

In offering Gaétan up, Michel had tried to make peace, peace instead of slaughter, but there would be none. In that moment, Christian had felt victorious, but it was short-lived and the rage he tried desperately to suppress continually threatened to consume him. Perhaps if Michel had cut out Gaétan's heart, he and Michel would have had a different life, but it was impossible to imagine any other path after all these centuries. The past was unchangeable, carved in stone with such clarity it felt like yesterday.

Did Gaétan hate him enough to come for them now? Was Lucien here at the request of Gabrielle or Solange? He reflected on the two beautiful vampires who had played such a powerful role in his life and the young mortal woman whom he had loved above all others.

Lost in his thoughts, Christian found himself at the entrance to Central Park South. Lucien and the other vampire had just crossed inside, into his domain. He knew every inch of the park; he had watched it grow and flourish for the past hundred years. *How ironic,* he thought, *to meet their death in my backyard!*

Chapter Three

⚜

AMANDA PERRETTI REACHED her office at the end of a narrow hallway in the cavernous European Sculpture and Decorative Arts department just as her telephone rang. Despite the fact that it was the Friday of the Fourth of July weekend, the Metropolitan Museum of Art remained opened until 8:45 PM. She had to get this e-mail out before leaving, and already there had been numerous interruptions. She headed toward her desk, which took up most of the tiny room, dodging piles of books on the floor. Her workday usually ended around six PM, unless she was working on a special exhibition. Tonight was one of those nights.

She accidentally knocked over an empty Styrofoam coffee cup perched precariously on one corner of her desk. A stack of books awaiting her perusal took up the rest of the available space. With a sigh, she settled back into her faux-leather chair. She glanced down at a book with the imposing title *Ancient Reliquaries*, opened to the chapter on French reliquaries of the ninth century, in preparation for the next exhibition. *Dare I try to read this tonight?*

After ignoring the first three rings, something compelled her to pick up her phone.

"Amanda Perretti," she said with a sigh, bringing the receiver to her ear without taking her eyes off her computer screen.

"Hey, it's me." It was a deep, familiar voice that evoked so much sadness for her.

"Ryan?"

"The one and only."

"How are you? Where are you?" She grabbed a pen and reached for one of several yellow legal pads buried underneath the catalogs and photographs that littered her desk and began doodling, an old habit from childhood.

"I'm in the park, over by the Boathouse."

"Ryan, it's been six months. Where have you been?"

Amanda flashed back to the first time she had walked into the Great Hall of the museum with her mother and brother, Ryan. She was ten. He was fourteen. Her mother had taken them to see a Seurat exhibition one hot summer day. Ryan complained the entire time they were there, but Amanda marveled at the architecture, the bustling crowds, and most of all, the art. She and her mother shared a love of art that transcended their volatile relationship. Ryan, on the other hand, hated the entire experience and refused to ever return.

Amanda had fallen in love with the Met and swore to work there one day. It had been two years since she had taken a job there, yet she still felt like that little girl, anticipating wandering through the European paintings gallery on the second floor, standing before the statues of Roman Gods on the first floor, or marveling at African masks in the Rockefeller Wing. It was her home, her most favorite place in the world.

"Hey listen, I was wondering . . ."

That's how it always began. She wouldn't hear from him for months, and then he would call, strung out and desperate. She could only imagine where he crashed and how he survived day to day, but somehow he always managed to find her.

With the phone against one ear, she began to straighten up her desk. As she slid aside the latest Eighteenth Century European Decorative Arts catalog, she exposed a photograph of the two of them with their father that she kept on her desk. Taken the Christmas before her thirteenth birthday, she and Ryan stood next to their artificial Christmas tree while her mom snapped away. Amanda was smiling, her arms wrapped around her dad's thin waist. Ryan was seventeen, sullen and already using drugs. Their mother had tried to keep their father's illness from them, but they knew the truth. Their mother only confided in them that he was terminally ill when he became noticeably thinner and weaker. One month later, he was dead.

Ryan locked himself in his bedroom, angry and withdrawn, while Amanda continued to be the straight-A student. Ryan had left home right after high school, and now Amanda rarely spoke with him unless he needed money or a place to crash for a few days.

"Let me guess, Ry?" She picked up a strand of her wavy hair and twirled it around her finger.

"Amanda, I . . . I need a couple bucks . . . I promise . . ."

"Spare me your promises, Ryan."

"Man, I'm grateful for whatever you could lend me." She scribbled a smiley face with a frown next to his name.

"Look, I have to take care of some things before I leave tonight. The best I can do is fifteen minutes, if you can wait that long." She checked her watch. It was ten PM.

"Sounds good," he slurred. "I'll be in front of the Boathouse." The receiver clicked.

Great, one of the most romantic places in New York and I'm meeting my drug-addicted brother who needs desperately to score. Framing the Lake in Central Park, the Loeb Boathouse, commonly known to New Yorkers as the Boathouse, consisted of an indoor restaurant with windows that looked out onto the lake. An outdoor patio and dock with rowboat rentals completed the scene. One could even rent a gondola. When Amanda fantasized about a dream date, the Boathouse figured in there somewhere, along with Bethesda Fountain, situated on the southern tip of the Lake.

The focal point of Central Park, Bethesda Fountain and Terrace was a meeting place all year long for tourists, couples, and families. On nice days, Amanda tried to get out of the museum to take her lunch break there. She loved staring up at the eight-foot bronze angel, alighting upon the fountain, holding a lily in one hand while blessing the water with the other. She never tired of sitting on the stone wall, watching the passing scene as weddings were conducted, tourists snapped photographs, celebrities sashayed past and New Yorkers on their lunch hour watched one another.

She imagined getting married there one day with Bethany as her bridesmaid—her only witness—and the groom? There was no one in her life right now, but she sensed he was close by and it was only a matter of fate until their paths crossed. *You hopeless romantic, Amanda,* she thought, finishing writing her e-mail. *The man you want doesn't exist.*

She straightened up the piles of books and notepads on her desk, tossed out her Styrofoam coffee cup from that morning, and grabbed her purse. It was Friday and the weekend could not start fast enough. *Just give him the money and go*, she thought as she exited the main entrance of the museum. She headed up Fifth Avenue and back into Central Park. A cool summer night, rare in New York, enveloped her as she headed down East Drive. It was still light, and people flooded into the park. She dodged bicyclists, rollerbladers, and joggers as she cross the 72nd Street Transverse heading south.

Her high heels clicked on the pavement as she walked along; thankful she had worn a cotton sweater. She and Bethany had plans to watch the fireworks tomorrow night and just relax over the holiday weekend. Work had been so hectic lately, and she needed to recharge her batteries with a good book and one of her favorite movies, *Dangerous Liaisons*.

Up ahead on her left, she noticed the Renaissance man, as she called him, playing beautiful music on a flute. She nodded as she passed. He smiled back and kept playing. She heard the din of the diners at the Boathouse as she turned right off East Drive, and scanned the crowd for her brother, wondering what he looked like these days. Something caught her eye as she passed a pedestrian tunnel, and suddenly there he was, hunched over on the steps leading down into the tunnel.

"Ryan?"

He stood up slowly and she felt herself swallow hard. He appeared gray in the street light, his eyes sunken and his skin broken out and sallow. His usual jeans and T-shirt were filthy, just like his dark hair. She tried to remember the older brother she loved and admired. The youthful beauty he was before the drugs had claimed him. Although he was four years older, they were often mistaken for twins, with the same wavy dark hair, dark green eyes, and angular faces. He was taller, taking after her mother's side of the family.

She tried to read him, pluck his thoughts out of the air like she used to, but it had become impossible. She promised herself she would give him all the money she had and would leave before they had a chance to fight again.

This time will be different, she thought, forcing a smile.

"Hey," he said with as sigh, reaching for her.

She felt herself stiffen in his embrace.

"How are you, Ryan?" She searched his face for a hint of the boy she remembered, but could find nothing, only a stranger, and a bag of bones who needed more than just a hot bath and a meal.

"Ah, you know, hanging in there. How's the museum? Are you still into all that blood and guts?" He gestured with his index finger across this throat.

She knew exactly what he meant. The French Revolution was her passion. She had learned even more from working on a recent exhibition titled *Jewelry of La Révolution Française*. The experience had culminated with her contact with one of rarest and most beautiful suites of jewelry to survive the destruction of the French aristocracy, a parure belonging to Marie Antoinette. Even as a child, she had been obsessed with the French Revolution. She never questioned her love of one of the bloodiest periods in modern history, nor thought it odd. Most of her family was of French ancestry. It was her mother, Catherine Richard, who had muddied the waters of her perfect French lineage by marrying an Italian.

Fascinated by both French history and her own genealogy, Amanda had researched her family tree back to a Monique Moulin, who had been born in California in 1842. She had married Charles Devereaux and come to New York at the turn of the century, where she died in 1901. Amanda knew nothing more about Monique except what a New York census could tell her. Her relatives were names and dates on a page, and for some reason the trail had gone cold with Monique. Though Amanda had no proof, she sensed her family had fled France and gone to England during the French Revolution.

"Where are you living?" She asked impulsively.

"There's this place in the West Village I've been hanging out—"

"A halfway house, I hope."

"Well not really." Ryan sighed and ran his hands through his hair. He began to walk toward the tunnel as a couple passed them. Amanda followed hesitantly.

"There's this club . . ." He stared straight ahead as he walked. "I give blood and I get paid so I can buy—"

"What do you mean, you give blood?" She stopped him. "Ryan, what the hell are you talking about?"

He seemed distracted, more distant than she remembered.

"Here." She reached into the side pocket of her leather purse for a fifty-dollar bill. "This is all I have."

"Thanks a lot, 'Man. You always come through for me." He gave her the same line every time.

"Yeah." She fought back tears, promising to make this short and sweet. "That's my lot in life, I guess. Always there for you."

There was so much she wanted to say, but then, what was the use of it?

"I'd better go now," he announced, giving her a weak smile.

"What are those marks, Ryan? She noticed marks on his neck, just below his left ear. They looked like puncture wounds.

"I told you I give blood to . . ." He reached up and touched the wounds.

"Ryan, who are these people you are hanging out with?"

"No, it's *what* are they . . . they're . . . beautiful and different, Amanda."

"Why don't you come home with me tonight, let me help—"

"I gotta get back. One of them owes me money. He promised to pay me later."

"Where is this place?" She ran her hand through her hair, something she did when she got angry. "Who are these people?"

"You wouldn't believe me if I told you, baby sister. I am well taken care of." He glanced off into space, and at that moment Amanda felt afraid for him. There had been a time when they could read each other's thoughts, and then it had stopped. She blamed it on the drugs.

"You don't appear to be well taken care of, Ryan. Let me get you cleaned up and—"

"I can't, Amanda. I give them my blood and . . . it doesn't hurt and—"

"Ryan, you aren't making sense. Why would anyone take your blood?"

"They are vampires, man. In fact, the guy I was just with was asking about you. He musta read my mind."

At that moment, she thought he was delusional. Later she would think about their conversation often, replaying it in her mind.

"Ryan, you aren't making any sense." Panic gripped her as he pulled away.

"You're a great sister." He smiled and tried to hug her again. "I gotta go."

"Fine. Keep in touch." She choked back tears.

Their eyes locked, and for brief second she recognized him, which made the moment all the more painful. She turned, listening to her footsteps on the pavement. Amanda tried to put him out of her mind. It wasn't like she was responsible for him, but he always haunted her. She was almost out of the tunnel when she decided to turn back. Maybe she could catch him, and maybe it could be different this time.

Suddenly, the echo of his screams filled the tunnel.

"Ryan?" She ran back into the darkness, away from the crowds at the Boathouse.

In the streetlight she saw them, but it took a second for her mind to wrap around what was happening. Ryan was flailing, pinned up against the wall, held up by his throat by a tall figure in dark clothes. It took her another second to realize that he was dangling about two feet off the ground.

"Amanda, run!" Her brother screamed, flailing his arms and legs at the man who held him.

She heard a snarl and then the dark figure pulled out what looked like a hunting knife. Ryan tried to pummel the looming figure while she watched in horror as in one sweeping motion, he slit Ryan's throat from ear to ear. Ryan gurgled as blood poured down the front of his gray T-shirt, spreading out like a dark fan covering his chest. Amanda tried to scream as her brother was dropped to the ground in a heap, his blood gushing onto the sidewalk as the dark figure knelt over him. She felt something warm running down her leg and realized she had just wet herself. The murderer turned toward her, snarling through what looked like exposed fangs.

Sweat trickled down her face as he came toward her, catlike and graceful. Amanda tried to see his face in the shadows. She glanced at Ryan, not moving on the ground. *He's dead, oh my God, he's dead.* Her legs would not move; they felt like concrete. *I am going to die here with him.*

"Antoine, get away from her." A man's voice rang out. The figure turned toward the voice in the darkness.

Amanda heard a swooshing sound and froze, as Antoine's head separated from his neck, momentarily suspended in the air before dropping and rolling toward her brother. His body crumbled, falling on the pavement going up in flames. Everything seemed to happen in slow motion.

Another figure emerged from the shadows. He seemed shorter, with shoulder-length brown hair. Like the other man, he too was dressed in black. He hovered over her brother's body, dabbed Ryan's blood onto his finger, and licked it, like a cat lapping a bowl of milk.

Oh my God. She heard the words echo in her head, but had she said them aloud? *Is he going to kill me, too?*

He hovered over her brother's body for what seemed like forever. Amanda watched him, wondering what he was doing, then he looked up at her and snarled, slowly getting up off the ground, his face covered in Ryan's blood. He had something in his hand, a jar perhaps, that he shoved into the inside pocket of his coat.

"There you are my beauty. Come to me, child." He called to her in a voice that caressed her, and it seemed as if he recognized her. She could not hear his footsteps as he came toward her. It was as if he floated above the concrete. He reached out his hand, and she saw his eyes, dark and bottomless. Something caught her eye as another figure came out of the shadows. He was tall and thin, and wore a flowing black coat. She noticed that his golden hair hung down his back in flowing waves. He was beautiful, and she sensed he would not harm her.

"Get away from her, Lucien, unless you want your head to roll," the blond man hissed vehemently, his deep voice strangely comforting.

He gracefully stepped toward her. Sweat trickled down her face as he studied her. It seemed as though he were making sure she was okay.

The other one hissed at the tall blond figure. Then he was gone, melting into the evening shadows. She stood alone with the mysterious man. She wanted to thank him, but then she noticed the bloody machete in his right hand. *Is he going to take my head, too?* She felt weak as darkness descended.

Chapter Four

GAÉTAN STOOD AT the salon window of the apartment he had once shared with Gabrielle and stared down at the Saturday night traffic on the Rue de Rivoli. The lights illuminating the Louvre reflected back into the room. This had been his residence since the turn of the nineteenth century, when La Révolution Française had finally ended and the arrogant Napoleon had come to power. Gaétan folded his arms across his muscular chest and debated whether summoning Gabrielle had been a good idea. They had not spoken since the night he brought Solange back to Paris in 1814. Taking Solange as his lover had infuriated Gabrielle, and had been the final blow to their already stormy relationship. To this day, they shared the city in an uneasy truce. *Yet she has agreed to come here tonight.*

He listened for Solange's return from the Bois de Boulogne. She had gone hunting in the park for the usual fare: a prostitute, a drug addict, or one of Paris's many homeless. The Bois was one kind of park by day and an infamous red-light district by night. Prostitutes were a dime a dozen; easy prey for his kind. He had not told her about the meeting, fearing her typical reaction: rage. He ran his hand through his sandy brown hair and fought his own hunger. Though he was older and needed less blood to survive, tonight's meeting worried him and he could not afford to lose his focus. A quick drink would take the edge off, but there was little time to hunt. *Just a sip*, he thought, fighting the urge.

He threw open the French doors and breathed in the late summer air. His sense of urgency grew with each passing night. A warm breeze blew his shoulder-length hair away from his chiseled face and creamy skin. Lucien had returned to him and reported that Antoine had slit the young mortal's throat, but paid with his own life. Lucien had barely escaped with his own life, yet he had done the unthinkable. He had taken blood from the dead mortal, scooping it up into a vial before the retched Christian had chased him away. When he dangled the blood in front of Gaétan, the older vampire saw no other way. Luring him into the Bois, he had chained him and left him to die in the late summer sun, not before he learned where Lucien had hid the precious blood. When he returned two days later, only ashes remained.

Gaétan reached for the warm vial around his neck and shut the window. He appeared odd, surrounded by feminine finery; the room had been decorated by Solange in Chintz draperies, upholstered chairs, white overflowing book cases, and a white marble mantle adorned with English porcelains. Even the oriental carpet was in pink and blue hues.

He dashed into the masculine master bathroom. Turning on the hot tap, he methodically removed his Rolex watch and numerous silver rings as the sink filled up. Bending over the bowl, Gaétan splashed hot water on his face in an attempt to calm himself and to focus on the task at hand. A million thoughts raced through his mind, most revolving around the vial of blood dangling at his neck.

Solange had been a child when he had seen her for the first time, after following Christian and Michel to London. He had to admit that he had been just as curious about her as was Gabrielle. In all his life, Gaétan knew of only one instance in which a mortal and a vampire had produced a child; that child had died shortly after birth. But Solange had been a miracle. He had kept a watchful distance, intrigued by Christian and Michel's roles in her life, as well as the little girl.

As he dried his face, he recalled going back and forth between Paris and London under the resentful eyes of Gabrielle, as Christian and Michel had settled into a new life in London and Solange had grown up. Many French aristocrats had fled there out of necessity, yet he found the city unimaginative and boorish. He squirted on his favorite French cologne and studied himself in the bedroom mirror. *It is only Gabrielle you fool, so why are you preening like a teenager on his first date?*

Black jeans hugged his thin, muscular legs, and his black shirt lay tucked in at his narrow waist. His black Harley Davidson boots with silver buckles and a high heel gave him the illusion of being taller than his 5'8" frame. Let Solange comb Rue du Rivoli and Avenue Foch for haute couture. He preferred jeans and a T-shirt to the ruffles, great coats, and knickers of centuries past.

He took the vial from around his neck and buried it in his dresser drawer beneath his neatly folded socks. Then, changing his mind, he impulsively grabbed it from the drawer, twisted off the cap, and tapped the vial on his tongue. *Easy there, just a little this time.* The warm blood oozed down his throat, igniting a fire in his veins.

Gaétan sat down on the king-size bed, suddenly dizzy; his head reeled with the now-familiar images from the boy's life.

He lay back and closed his eyes, clutching the sheets as a kaleidoscope of sights and sounds filled his head in a rush. The vampire felt his limbs melt into the mattress as his senses heightened, yet his mind felt calm and at peace. *I have not felt this way since I was a mortal man*, he thought as the blood inside him brought forth the mortality he had long ago lost and strangely missed.

He rolled onto his side and clutched his stomach as pain burst through his guts. He broke out in a sweat, feeling weak and vulnerable. He knew it would pass and the feeling of humanity rather than his predatory nature as a bloodsucker would fill him up. He felt inhumanly powerful, yet mortal again; a hypnotic, seductive combination of sensations.

The images of a young girl morphed into a beautiful woman, both elegant and erotic. She stood with her brother in the park, the night he was murdered. He could see the worry and fear on her face. He fought his erection and ejaculation as her voice and smell caressed him, wrapping him in feelings of acceptance, love, and comfort like nothing he had ever known. Her dark green eyes smiled up at him as she bent her neck for him to drink.

Whether it was the boy's blood causing these hallucinations or his heart, lonely and desperate for love, did not matter to the ancient vampire. Irrational or not, he had already made up his mind to go to New York to find her.

I don't care if Christian is guarding her night and day, he thought as he tried to sit up on the king-size bed. *She will be mine.*

Chapter Five

❧

GAÉTAN SAT UP and glanced at his watch. It was midnight. He jumped up to get ready for Gabrielle's visit. As he passed Solange's dressing table, he took note of all her perfumes, makeup, and jewelry haphazardly strewn on the tabletop. She never had been a neat person. Even as a young married woman living in London in the early nineteenth century, she had been a slob. Thankfully she had married well and had household servants. He picked up one of her hairbrushes and ran it under his nose. Just then he heard the lock click, the front door open and close. Like a cool breeze, she enveloped him in her thin arms wrapped around his waist. He let her hold him for a moment.

"You seem pensive of late, my love." She whispered into his back, her upper class British accent as sharp as a knife.

Gaétan closed his eyes, feeling her warm body engorged with blood from feeding pressed up against him. She would want to make love before their night at the opera, and afterward wander the Champs-Élysées until dawn.

She slipped past him and sat down at her makeup table to brush her thick, brown hair. Turning first one way and then another, she studied her impish profile in the mirror. Gaétan knew she was not sure if she liked either her new bob haircut or the highlights the Avenue Foch salon had convinced her were stylish and made her look younger. The torches burned low, giving her alabaster skin a yellowish tint. She applied a pale pink lipstick, and then blotted her full lips before brushing on mascara and a smoky brown eye shadow that accentuated her luminous brown eyes. Her high cheekbones were flushed from feeding.

She began to play with the chain of her heart-shaped necklace a gesture Gaétan knew meant she was impatient. Gaétan followed her into her walk-in closet but said nothing as she began flipping through the hangers, eyeing first one gown and then another. Finally she settled on a strapless black satin Dior.

"Solange, we must talk," he whispered, checking his watch again. Gabrielle would be there any minute. Taking the hanger out of her hand, he put it back on the rack. "We are not going to the opera tonight. Dress simply and meet me in the living room."

"What's going on, Gee?" She asked, using her nickname for him as she followed him into the living room. She was never one to take orders from anyone, even him, without an explanation.

"We have company coming tonight. I need you to be civil, listen, and keep your wits about you. Now please, Solange, get dressed."

She replied with her usual pout and folded her arms over her chest.

"Pray tell, Gee, who is—?"

Just then, the doorbell rang.

"It will be a surprise." He smiled and headed toward the foyer with a knot in his stomach. He knew how much she hated surprises.

Gaétan took a deep breath before opening the front door. He could feel them standing just inside the shadows on the pavement, visible to the vampire eye but never to mortals passing by. She stood in a long red gown. She looked just as he remembered her: wild, dark curly hair flowing over her broad shoulders, wide set dark eyes, fleshy lips, long legs, and voluminous breasts. It was not regret, he told himself, but nostalgia for the beautiful and tumultuous eighteenth century.

Then he noticed Étienne; tall and commanding, towering over Gabrielle. Like Solange, he had chosen the path of the nightwalker willingly. Although it was Christian and Michel who had found him on the streets of Paris, it was Gabrielle who had turned him, on his sixteenth birthday, before taking him as her lover. Gaétan wondered if she still pined away for her beloved Christian. *Is that why she has come?*

It was Étienne who first stepped into the light, dressed entirely in black. His once long hair was now cropped short, his blue eyes both woeful and intense. They reminded Gaétan of Christian's eyes; deep and bottomless, hypnotic and unyielding.

"We got your message." He spoke, his lips barely moving.

"Please come in, both of you." He turned both palms up in a common gesture meaning no malice. "It is only Solange and I."

Gabrielle stepped into the light next to Étienne. "How do we know you do not mean to slaughter us as well, Gaétan?" Gabrielle's voice wrapped around him, feeling painfully erotic and soothing, as it had always been between them.

31

"As I told you in my message, this affects us all. Please come upstairs."

Étienne stepped aside, allowing Gabrielle to go first, as her age and status dictated. Gaétan walked beside her into the foyer and up the long flight of stairs to the living room. He could barely hear her breathing as she floated up the stairs beside him. No sooner had they ascended the staircase than Solange appeared in the living room; her eyes dark and brooding.

"What are they doing here, Gee?" She recoiled, pressing herself up against the fireplace.

The two women glared at each other.

Gaétan stepped between them. He could hear their thoughts in his head, an effect of the potent blood he had ingested.

"Solange, I promised them no harm, do you understand? Gabrielle, Étienne, please sit down."

Étienne waited until Gabrielle was settled before positioning himself behind her. Gaétan watched his former lover glance nervously around the familiar living room, taking it all in. He took a seat in a large overstuffed chair opposite the couch and waited for the right moment to begin. He could sense their apprehension and fear.

"Thank you both for coming." Gaétan's voice was raspy yet soothing. "Several months ago, I began hearing talk about a mortal in New York City who had a different kind of blood, a blood that gave us atypical powers. At first I dismissed the gossip, but it persisted. I made inquiries to either substantiate these strange rumors or quell them completely. Solange met up with a vampire named Gilliam who had been in a club in New York and fed from a young mortal there."

Gaétan watched the masklike faces of the two vampires who sat opposite him for some sort of reaction, but he found none. Solange had taken to twirling a piece of her highlighted hair. He knew she was restless, like a caged lion. He feared her inability to restrain herself and noticed that Étienne watched her as well.

"Gilliam mentioned that this club, the Grey Wolf, is the hangout of Michel Baptiste and Christian Du Mauré." Gaétan sensed a slight shift in Gabrielle. He thought he saw her face soften in the low lights.

"I don't think it is any surprise that this mortal sought shelter in this club, under the auspices of Christian."

Gabrielle straightened the folds of her gown, which distracted him. Solange had come closer; she was now standing beside Gaétan. He fought the urge to swat her away.

"Is this fact, Gaétan, or merely speculation?" Gabrielle asked in a heavy French accent, her gaze drifting past him to Solange.

"We sent Antoine and Lucien to kill the mortal," Solange blurted out, a bold grin on her face. "Antoine lost his head, thanks to my father—"

Gaétan reached up and stroked her leg. "Solange, please keep your mouth shut."

She sat down at his feet like an obedient guard dog, closer now to Gabrielle.

"Solange speaks the truth. Not wanting this mortal's blood to get into the wrong hands, I sent Antoine and Lucien to do away with the boy. Christian ambushed them in Central Park, and although Antoine managed to slaughter the mortal, Christian took his head. Lucien went after the other one, but Christian drove him away."

"The other one?" Gabrielle blurted out impulsively.

Solange snapped. "Amanda, his sister."

"Amanda?" Gabrielle whispered, as the name wrapped around the vampire like a fog. "There are two of them?"

Gaétan focused on the murmur of traffic on the street below. A vision of Amanda filled his head as he fought another erection. Étienne shifted slightly, his leather coat rubbing against the leather couch cushion.

"What proof did you have that this boy's blood was such a threat?" He asked timidly. "Christian has been chasing these mortals for decades. Why the sudden panic?"

"Good point. Gaétan, you mention blood falling into the wrong hands. Whose might those be?" Gabrielle smiled and turned her dark eyes on him. She folded her hands in her lap. Gaétan knew she was hiding her anger, trying to remain calm.

"Lucien said the boy needed money for drugs and was offering himself up to anyone. He said drinking from him was like nothing he had ever tasted. It more than fed his craving; it had a power all its own. When I pressed him, he could not describe the sensations. I believe the word he used was ineffable. His said that his vampiric nature acquiesced to his mortal self and the sensation of the two opposite worlds blending was beyond imagination."

"Where is Lucien? I would question him myself."

"Funny, but he hasn't been around lately." Solange said with a shrug as she ran her hand slowly up and down Gaétan's calf.

Gabrielle met his stare and Gaétan knew she was probing. He quickly glanced past her toward the book case.

Étienne leaned forward. "I don't quite understand the threat, Gaétan."

Gaétan ran his hand through his hair, debating whether to tell them any more of the powers in the blood. Étienne continued to stare as more thoughts took form.

"This boy was a perceived threat to you, and you took care of it, Gaétan. What is the need for this meeting?" He leaned even closer to the older vampire.

"My father is watching over Amanda like a bull in heat," Solange blurted out, still rubbing her lover's calf, arousing Gaétan despite his focus.

"Enough, Solange," Gaétan whispered, rubbing her head.

"Oh, come on, Gee, he wants her blood for himself, that selfish bastard. Then he will become all-powerful and try to reclaim Paris again." Solange smiled up at her lover.

Gabrielle jumped up. "You impudent brat! Have you no manners, no self-control? I cannot believe you are your father's daughter. If he is protecting her, it is not for her blood. It is to keep her away from monsters like you."

Solange rose to her feet as well. "You make my father out to be so goddamned noble and high-minded. Where was he when I was dying?"

"You stupid girl." Gabrielle hissed, stepping closer to her. Étienne placed his hand on her shoulder and she stepped back, composing herself.

"What is it that you want from us, Gaétan?" Gabrielle snarled, her usual composure beginning to erode.

"I am worried that Christian is keeping the girl for himself and that if he does take her, he will become powerful enough to return home and slaughter us, taking control of this city."

"I can't believe you are suggesting such a thing. All he has ever wanted is to be left alone. Why can't you let your hatred and jealousy of him go for Christ's sake?"

"I fear for us, Gabrielle. If he could behead Antoine, there is no telling what he would do to you or me." Gaétan smiled, his dimpled cheeks and full lips changing his entire face, giving him a warm, welcoming presence. He dared step closer to his former lover.

Étienne stepped between them, feeling the need to defend his old friend. "He has made no contact with us for centuries, and we have worked hard for this truce. Why do you think he would suddenly want to hunt us down now?"

How could he tell them the truth? He killed Lucien and took the jar of the mortals' blood for himself, that he wanted Amanda like nothing else in his life. He was packed and ready to leave Paris. None of them would try to stop him, and only Solange would want to tag along. She had always been curious about Christian, but the last thing he wanted was her with him in New York. This was something he needed to do alone, and perhaps with their blessing he could carry out his plan. Gaétan sat back down.

"There is something I have not told you both."

Gabrielle and Étienne took his lead and sat down, while Solange lingered back near the fireplace watching them. Gaétan studied Gabrielle as she never took her eyes off Solange.

"This blood gives a vampire the ability to walk in the daylight hours, impervious to the sun's rays."

Étienne jumped up off the couch. "Is this a joke?"

"I wish it were," Gaétan lied, trying to conceal his own dependency on the blood from them, looking past them with feigned worry.

"Lucien told you this... ... he experienced walking in . . . living and breathing during the day?" Gabrielle shook her head in shock.

"This is what he said." Gaétan shrugged, thinking back to the morning after the first night he had tasted Ryan's blood. Solange had already drifted off to sleep, and he too had felt the dawn approaching and sleep descending just as it had every day for the past four hundred and fifty years. Then, just as the sun rose over the Louvre, the feeling had lifted. He stood at his living room window as the sun bathed the room in light, covering his skin and hair in a yellow glow, caressing him in warmth. *Yes, it is ineffable . . .*

Étienne sat back down on the couch. "There are those that would view this blood as a gift and others who would see it as an abomination, a horror."

"Exactly, and if Christian can walk during the day, he becomes a god with an advantage over all of us." Gaétan was suddenly on his feet. "I need to destroy this mortal girl before someone else finds out about her."

"Or my father takes her for himself," Solange snarled. "Kill them both, Gaétan." She rubbed up against him like a cat rubbing up against its owner's leg for affection.

Gabrielle was off the couch as well. "Christian would never harm her, you fool. He has such an exaggerated sense of right and wrong . . . trust me. She is safest with him and Michel."

Solange rubbed up against Gaétan again. "Bring the one called Michel, the dark one back for me. I want to taste him."

"Why don't you send Philippe or one of your other lackeys?" Gabrielle asked, trying to control her anger.

"Exactly, my love. Why do you have to go?" Solange grinned from ear to ear as she wrapped her arms around his legs.

"Look what happened to Antoine!" He shrugged innocently. "I thought he could do the job and he was slaughtered."

"Perhaps he just wants to protect the girl," Étienne chimed in. "I cannot imagine Christian using her for his own gain."

"We have no idea who he is anymore, Étienne. Who knows what he thinks these days."

"If killing the girl means keeping the peace here, then you have my consent, but that is all, Gaétan." Gabrielle waved a long finger at him. "Anything more I will view as a declaration of war, and I doubt either of us is up to it."

"Thank you Gabrielle."

"How much time do you need?" Gabrielle asked curtly.

"Give me six months." He smiled into her dark eyes and took her hands. "I promise you I will return with her head."

"I trust your word on this, Gaétan. No harm to Christian or Michel."

For a moment, the walls dropped between them. The centuries of bloodshed and pain vanished, and he felt her as she must have been as a mortal woman, centuries before he had met her. *It is the blood*, he thought, still holding her hands.

"I thank you both for coming." Gaétan escorted them to the door with a pang of regret when they were gone.

Her perfume lingered in the living room.

"Please come to bed, Gee." Solange whispered, running her hand over his crotch. She wrapped herself around him. He could feel her need, her desperation as she tried to arouse him, but he was already gone, lost in the sights and smells of his new home, New York.

PART TWO
NEW YORK - SIX MONTHS LATER

Chapter Six

IT BEGAN TO snow just as Amanda left the museum for the night. She headed down the stately front steps and crossed Fifth towards Park Avenue. After returning a skirt she felt she could not afford, she decided to see if Detective Ross was in his office. It had been six months since her brother's death and two months since she had heard from anyone at the NYPD. As she headed back toward the Central Park precinct, she studied the faces of the passersby out of habit, forever searching for the stranger who had saved her life. *I may never see him again, but I will never forget him,* she thought, dodging the sidewalk full of rush hour commuters.

The last six months of her life felt like a dream. After the attack, she had spent the weekend in St. Vincent's hospital being treated for shock. Since then, she had continually relived the events in the park, trying to make sense of it all. Bethany Daniels, her best friend and roommate, professed to believe her descriptions of Ryan's murderer—a madman with fangs and a knife—and the tall blond-haired man wielding a machete. She wondered if Bethany was simply humoring her. The road back to her normally sedate life had been rocky at best, and the disturbing memories of that night continually haunted her.

Her cell phone rang, interrupting her ruminations. Glancing at the incoming number, she smiled. It was Thomas, a night shift guard in the European Decorative Arts and Sculpture galleries. She had noticed him one night about five months ago. Whenever Amanda found herself working late on exhibitions, they always managed to run into each other and he would say hi. One night she was on break, sipping a cup of coffee in the cafeteria, when he happened to come in on his break, too. From then on, whenever she worked late, they somehow managed to end up in the cafeteria at the same time. He would join her while as she ate a quick dinner or had a drink, but his visits were always brief.

As they got to know each other, they scheduled their breaks together. It seemed as if he had the uncanny ability to know when she needed a break, usually inviting her for a cup of coffee in the museum cafeteria just when it felt like her eyes would fall out of her head and she could not type or read another word. Sometimes he would translate French texts for her, and although she insisted on buying him dinner, he always refused, telling her how glad he was just to help her out.

"How's my favorite researcher?" A sultry male voice asked her.

"TGIF." She smiled to herself as she crossed over Park Avenue and headed back toward Fifth.

"My God, Cole doesn't have you guys working on the dinner dance yet?"

She dared not tell him that Cole Thierry, her boss, had scheduled their first staff meeting about the infamous April dinner dance that afternoon.

"Hey, it just started snowing, it's so beautiful." There was something about the snow that hypnotized her, although it reminded her of her father's death on a March day over a decade ago.

"I'll take another look at that book on Monday night. I stopped by, but you were gone already."

Amanda had found an old French volume under some papers on her desk. It was not the first time she had inexplicably discovered a book on her desk that was useful to her current research project. Whenever she showed one of these books to Thomas, he would close his eyes and hold the book to his forehead as if he could magically discern its contents. Then she would hand him a pair of gloves and he would open it carefully, his long thin hands gently turning each page as if he were caressing a lover. No one in her department could figure out where the volumes came from, and they disappeared just a mysteriously, as if the lender knew when she was finished with them.

Working together had brought Amanda and Thomas together professionally, and she had felt an instant attraction between them, but she was keeping her distance. They had an easy rapport, but she had been distracted, not sleeping well, and lost inside herself. *Is it me,* she thought, approaching the precinct. *Am I just too fragile and distracted, or is it that I keep holding out for him?*

"Thanks again, Thomas."

"Any plans tonight?"

She was so tired of having none, yet too honest to lie to him. "No, just thought I would take it easy. Maybe I'll rent a movie."

"Listen, Amanda," he said with a sigh, "I would love to take you out sometime. I haven't pushed . . . I figured you needed time."

She slowed down as she turned onto 84th Street.

"Is it that obvious?" She felt tears well up. "I guess it would be naïve of me to think you hadn't heard the gossip about my brother's murder. Everyone talks, I know, but it's . . ." She took a deep breath. "It's not something I talk much about."

"I don't want to upset you—"

"No, it's just so . . . It feels like a bad dream that I keep hoping to wake up from, but I don't—"

"I'm sorry for bringing it up, Amanda. The last thing I want to do is push you away from me."

She felt her knees buckle as his voice, with just a trace of a French accent, caressed her.

"It's not you, Thomas," she said with a sigh. "I'm just so distracted."

"I don't want to lose your friendship mon cherie."

"You won't, Thomas. It's just . . . There's so much about my brother's murder that's unresolved for me, and I can't seem to focus on much else. Call me obsessed."

"Even the obsessed need to go out dancing."

It had been so long since she had been on a date with anyone. Even before Ryan's murder, she had rebuffed an intern in the legal department. Maybe if she went out and got her mind off her brother and the mysterious stranger, she might have a good time. *Why can't I stop thinking about him?* She stared up at the street lamps and watched the falling snow, illuminated by the city lights.

"Amanda, are you there?"

She desperately needed to feel wanted, desirable. The stern face of the blond stranger loomed in her mind's eye. Then she thought about Thomas, with his bright brown eyes and dimpled cheeks. When he smiled, his face lit up. *What harm could come of one date?*

"I'm here, Thomas," she whispered into the phone.

"There's a dance club over on First Avenue and 54th called Zero Hour. Why not meet me there tomorrow night for a drink. Say eleven? I happen to have the night off."

Silence.

"I'll tell you what. I'll be there if you decide to come. Otherwise, no hard feelings and I'll see you next week."

"Thanks, Thomas. I'll think about it."

"Have a good weekend."

Thomas had a habit of never saying good-bye when they spoke. She stood at the doors of the Central Park precinct, not sure whether coming here had been a good idea. *Just go home, Amanda. Watch a movie and go out with Thomas tomorrow night. Try to have a normal life.*

With her hand on the door of the historic building, she turned to go home and then thought better of it.

I have to know the truth.

"Can I help you?" Quipped a burly police officer seated at a counter behind a Plexi-glass window.

"Yes, Detective Ross, please."

"Is he expecting you?" Officer Rizzo asked, getting up. Amanda stared into steely blue eyes surrounded by a fleshy face.

"He was handling the investigation of my brother's murder last July."

"Lady, we got lots of murders here. What's the name?"

"Perretti. Amanda Perretti. My brother's name was Ryan." Without being asked, she held up her picture ID from the Met.

She watched him pick up a black phone. She checked her watch: seven o'clock on a Friday night. It was doubtful he was in, but something had compelled her to stop by.

"Come on in." The glass door clicked open and Amanda entered the busy front desk area of the station. "Follow me."

She followed him down a narrow, dimly lit hallway, past a row of empty desks. He stopped at the last door on the right. *Will he remember me?* she wondered, taking a deep breath. Though they had spoken on the phone numerous times, she had met Ross only twice. Once when he questioned her in the hospital, and once in a coffee shop near her apartment. Rizzo knocked gently and opened the door for her. She slipped through the door into the office. The first thing that struck her was the darkness. Ross was sitting at his desk, feet up, sprinkled in long shadows cast from the desk lamp. She followed his legs down to his feet toward the shadows. *Someone else is here,* she sensed, shutting the door behind her. *He's not alone.*

"Ms. Perretti—" He swung his legs off the desk, coming towards her. He looked comfortable in a pair of black jeans, and a T-shirt. His hair was short and gelled. He looked less like a police officer and more like a GQ model. He came around the desk and extended his hand as if he were trying to prevent her from coming any farther into the room.

"Hi, Detective. I wasn't sure if you would remember me." She shook his hand. "I took a chance you might be in." She scanned the room, thinking it odd that he would sit in almost total darkness. It was such a contrast to the outer precinct, with its glaring fluorescent lights. She walked slowly toward him, eyeing the chair right in front of his desk.

"If this is a bad time, I can come back. I just got off work and I was wondering if there was anything new with my brother Ryan's murder . . ."

Something caught her eye as the shadows parted, as if releasing him reluctantly. He was taller than she remembered, probably 6'4" and reed thin, with dark, piercing eyes. Amanda clutched her purse as if the reality of his presence would knock her over. His wavy blonde hair flowed to his waist over a dark leather coat.

"Hello." He nodded, his deep voice holding her spellbound.

Amanda felt the floor shift and her body flush as she stared into his bottomless eyes. Thoughts filled her head, random, disconnected images of Paris, the French Revolution and lots of blood.

"Ms. Perretti, this is Christian."

"Hi." She thought she replied then realized she was holding her breath. She was transfixed, unable to look away, still not certain if he were a hallucination. A rush of adrenaline surged through her as his gaze hit something ethereal. It felt as though he could see into her soul.

"She works at the Metropolitan Museum of Art." Ross muttered hesitantly.

"Did you ever catch Lucien?" Amanda could not help but ask, riveted to his face, glad of the darkness. *It's really him.*

"Excuse me?" He whispered, his dark eyes darting nervously. His accent was French and thick.

"I remember you in the tunnel."

Amanda thought it took courage to say it aloud, not caring if either of them thought she was crazy.

"I doubt our paths have crossed." He smiled, quickly glancing at Ross. "You have business with the detective. I'd better go."

"You were brave, taking his head and saving my life."

"I don't know what you are talking about, Mademoiselle," he whispered.

"Ms. Perretti, please sit down. Let me take your coat," Detective Ross interrupted, gesturing toward a chair for her. Amanda could not move; she stood rooted to the spot.

"I have been looking for you for the past six months." The image of a large gray wolf running across a snow-covered landscape suddenly floated into her head. "No one believed me, but here you are. Detective, this is the man—"

"I must be going, Amanda."

Ross gestured toward the chair in front of his desk. "What can I do for you, Ms. Perretti?"

Christian forced a smile and strode toward the door in one graceful movement, his great coat flowing behind him. He was gone before she noticed the office door open and close.

"Wait." She called after him and ran down the hallway toward the front desk, but paused when she realized he was not in front of her. There was no way he could have left the building that fast. She turned and headed back down the hallway toward Ross's office. Maybe there was another exit.

Nothing. *Where did he go?*

Still wearing her coat, she reentered the detective's office to find Ross sitting behind his desk. Out of breath, she finally sat down.

"I know what I saw and I swear he was the man in the tunnel. He had some kind of knife and he . . ." She ran her fingers through her hair. "Please just tell me his last name, give me his address or a phone number."

"The best I can do is to give him your phone number. Whether he contacts you is his business." Ross shrugged. "Amanda, we have pursued all the leads, but we have nothing right now. There were no witnesses to corroborate your story. You were lying on the grass outside the tunnel, away from the murder scene. We can't explain how you got there."

"You don't understand. I need to speak to him." She leaned forward in her chair. "Please, Detective, he's the key. The only thing that has kept me going is the thought that he's out there."

"Ryan's killer will be found." Ross sat back in his chair.

"He was a homeless drug addict. He can't be your priority. Please, Detective."

"I am doing my best, Ms. Perretti."

"Someone slit my brother's throat and left him to bleed to death. I would be dead now if not for that man.... Christian."

Amanda thought it strange that she suddenly had a name for the beautiful stranger. She had almost turned back yet something had told her to come here tonight. She knew Ross was lying, though why, she had no idea. The two were obviously acquaintances, but what was he protecting?

Amanda remembered Ross being there when she awoke in the ER. He had questioned her repeatedly. He told her about the couple from England who had stumbled upon both she and Ryan. Her description of Ryan's murder, including monsters with fangs and men wielding machetes, seemed to be the stuff of horror movies and nightmares, explained to her as a delusion, shock brought on by seeing her brother murdered so violently.

When she had asked the police why she was still alive, they had no answers, only conjecture that the couple had scared the murderer away before he could get to her. There was no motive in her brother's death. The fifty dollars she had given him earlier was still in his front pocket.

"Let me pull the report. Perhaps there's some new development." Ross stood up. "I'll be right back, okay?"

Once alone Amanda stood up to slip off her heavy woolen coat when she accidentally stepped on something. Bending down, she retrieved a matchbook from behind the leg of her chair. *Did he drop these or were they left here?* She turned it over repeatedly under the desk lamp. At first it looked blank and then a gray silhouette of a wolf's face stared back at her. In tiny red letters, the words *Bleeker Street* loomed up at her. As she replayed the conversation with Christian over in her mind, a stunning realization hit her.

He used my first name. How did he know my first name?

She shoved the book of matches in her coat pocket and sat down just as Ross returned, carrying the file with him. While Ross talked at her, she pretended to listen. Beneath the coat draped across her lap, she texted Bethany, making plans to go down to the Grey Wolf tonight. It almost felt impossible that they finally met up. He felt like a dream, yet here he was, a living, breathing man.

She clutched the matchbox, determined to see him again.

If he's there, I'll find him, she thought, determined not to give up just yet.

Chapter Seven

CHRISTIAN LOVED WALKING in the falling snow. It was too early to go down to the Grey Wolf, and he needed to clear his head. Running into Amanda Perretti had rattled him. Although he could not discern whether it was carelessness or fate that had brought them together, he knew that being that close to her was too dangerous. He crossed the Great Lawn and headed to his favorite spot, Bethesda Terrace. Central Park had been a popular hunting ground for his kind since the turn of the century. Derelicts, drug addicts, runaways, and other assorted misfits were easy prey and never missed.

The cool steel of the machete against his back reminded him that it had been six months since the attack on Ryan and still nothing. Christian knew they would come again. It was just a question of when. Since Lucien had escaped him and returned to Paris, it would not be him this time. Someone unfamiliar, a bloodsucker he did not recognize, would try to take Amanda; the only one left.

He stopped on the steps of the terrace overlooking Bethesda Fountain and the Boathouse. The solitude was comforting, the view forever breathtaking, especially in the almost full moonlight.

Leaning against the stone wall, he listened to the distant traffic. With fewer mortals here and more hours of darkness, he felt as if he owned the park. Christian admired the architecture; the cast iron art nouveau lamp posts looked beautiful in the falling snow.

He usually came here alone. He was sometimes able to cajole Michel into joining him, but that usually meant the payback of a shopping spree on Madison Avenue or down in the East Village. This was his oasis, a place that never lost its allure. He would sit on the ornately carved stone steps of the terrace and stare down at Bethesda Fountain, marveling at its beauty in the moonlight, staring into the dark water while the mortal world passed by just as it always had done.

The Upper East Side and Central Park reminded him of the Paris he had left behind centuries ago. *All this beauty*, he thought, *and no one to share it with me.* On the rare occasion that he allowed himself to feel his own isolation, it overwhelmed him. The last woman he loved had died over two hundred years ago. Christian had cut off the part of himself that needed to love and receive it in return, although he remembered that he had once been a human being with fears, needs, and pain in his life. He had hungers beyond blood, and although there had been other women, his happiest and most painful memories lingered with Josette Delacore. *I am pitiful*, he thought, *and so very alone. If only I could be more like Michel, who just beds them and leaves them.*

"Come on, mon ami, just one more time?" Michel pleaded, dismounting in the courtyard of Christian's manor house one hot summer evening and handing the reins of his horse to one of the faceless servants who approached him.

"I told you, Michel, I'm not interested in whoring tonight," Christian explained, waiting for his friend near the well. He splashed water from the bucket onto his face, and then wiped the sweat from his eyes and took a long drink. "I am marrying Leila this fall, remember? I told you, no more." He took off his linen shirt and dropped it in the dirt before pouring water down his thin chest.

Michel watched him in silence.

"Ah, that feels good," Christian sighed, pouring a ladle of water down his back as the dirt pooled at his feet. He had just finished helping his father in the blazing June sun. All he wanted to do was eat dinner and go to bed. He spilled more water onto his blistered feet. In typical fashion, Michel had ridden up, dressed for a night of drinking and carousing with the local prostitutes.

"You have your whole life to be married to my sister." He reminded Christian. "How can you bed one woman for the rest of your life?"

"I am marrying her, not you," Christian scowled. He surveyed the one-story estate with the mansard roof that was his home. Despite the talk of riots in Paris, he still loved his country.

"This is hell, my friend. Paris is where we should go, before we are too old to enjoy ourselves."

Christian gazed at Michel, dressed in his finest cotton trousers, his white linen shirt, and a light green frock coat, frayed at the cuffs. His long dark hair hung loose around his shoulders, framing his high cheekbones and light green eyes. He was the most beautiful man Christian had ever seen, almost identical looking to his older sister.

Perhaps he would end up in Paris after all. He was more suited to a life of carousing than to a life in the countryside.

"Come on." Michel picked Christian's shirt up off the ground and tossed it at him. "You have your whole life to be a married man. Just for this summer stay a wild young man with me."

He though it odd that Michel suggested they contact Gabrielle. Michel had so easily fallen under her spell all those centuries ago when they were just young men. *I guess it is only fitting that he still believes she cares about us.* Christian had tried to forget her. Despite not trusting her, the three of them would forever remain connected by blood.

The snow fell harder, reminding him of the night his life changed forever. They had met Gabrielle the previous summer at the chateau of friends. He and Michel had seen her mingling with the crowd, weaving from guest to guest. Neither of them had recognized the beautiful woman, laughing and talking, her dark eyes smiling. She wore a purple silk dress that shimmered in the candlelight, complimenting her pale skin. Her shiny black hair was piled high on her head. Eventually she made her way over to them.

After making polite conversation, Michel had convinced her to come home with them both. Christian fondly remembered the three of them fornicating until dawn, when he and Michel passed out from sheer exhaustion. *If only it had ended that night*, Christian thought, still staring down at the fountain. She came to them night after night until they became more than a ménage a trois. They were inseparable as summer turned to fall and then to winter.

Why is it that the most profound events in our lives creep up on us without warning, Christian thought, remembering the March night when his life changed forever. It had started as a typical day on their estate in Meudon, France. Christian and his brother, Guillaume, lived alone with their father. Their mother had died when Christian was a child, taken by the pox.

Christian walked down the long set of steps to Bethesda Fountain, tracing his footsteps in the snow, and thought back to his only ever fight with Michel. He had given Michel an ultimatum—had forced him to decide between their lifelong friendship and the woman Christian feared was coming between them. He felt it should end, but Michel would not hear of it, and so Christian had cut him off, swearing only to see Michel when he had made his decision.

Christian was out in the stables with his prized black mare, Starlight. He generally did his best thinking while working. Despite the cold, he found himself in the stables bailing hay and cleaning out Starlight's stall. He was humming to himself when something made him turn around. Michel and Gabrielle stood framed in the doorway. Something about their posture, their hesitancy, alarmed Christian. He grabbed a lantern and slowly came toward them, wiping the sweat from his brow.

"What are you doing here? I told you not to come back until—" He began, staring into the dark eyes of his best friend. Gabrielle remained expressionless; her face flushed as it usually was after the three of them made love together.

Michel spoke, but his voice seemed distant, as if his lips were not moving. The sound was coming from somewhere far away. "I came to say goodbye my friend."

Michel's words made the hair on the back of his neck stand up. Something in his beautiful face terrified Christian. His skin looked like alabaster and his light green eyes were dark and vacuous.

"So, you have chosen her I see." Christian fought tears. "I suppose years of friendship means nothing to you."

He studied Michel's eyes for some response and found none.

"We can have each other, Christian, and Gabrielle too. We three can be together forever."

"What have you done to him?" Christian shone the lantern close to her face. Rage filled him at the thought of this woman taking control of his closest companion. As if sensing his anger, Gabrielle stepped behind Michel.

"Tell him, Michel. Tell him what I am and what you have chosen to become." She pulled him closer.

"What have you done, Michel?" He tried to shake his friend, but Michel felt like a rock and would not budge. He smelled of blood and dirt, as if he had been sleeping on the forest floor.

"Gabrielle is a vampire, Christian," Michel explained in a voice barely above a whisper. "And I have chosen to . . . join her."

For a moment, no one spoke or moved.

"You are *what?*" Christian asked, backing away and making the sign of the cross as he mumbled prayers.

"I have chosen eternity. I will live beyond this stinking, dirty place."

He reached out for Christian, who fell backwards and almost dropped the lantern.

"We can barely survive the taxes the king levees on us. Look at you, Christian, so young and handsome, but soon you will die and for what? I have chosen the God of immortality."

"You are talking crazy, Michel. Louis is our king. This is our home."

"I love you dearly, my friend. You too can have the gift Gabrielle has given me. Think of it, Christian. We can live beyond this place. I am free, my friend, free through a gift beyond our imagination. We can be time travelers, together forever!"

Michel reached into his jacket and pulled out a gleaming dagger. He sliced his arm, and Christian watched as his blood welled up and then stopped oozing. The cut closed up as if it had never been there at all. Christian crossed himself again.

"And what if I say no, will you kill me?" Christian asked, unable to comprehend the reality of the situation.

"We go to Paris to meet up with more of our kind," Gabrielle interjected. "We say good-bye tonight after I erase your memory of us. It is better this way."

"No, Michel," Christian cried out. "Please, do not leave me here."

Hot tears ran down his face. He was embarrassed to be weeping like a woman in front of Gabrielle, yet unable to imagine his life without Michel. How could he have no memory of his best friend? Christian could not bear it. He surrendered the lantern to Gabrielle as she gestured for him to lie down in the hay. Christian closed his eyes as the cold lips of his best friend brushed his cheek and Michel touched his face.

"Come with me." He whispered, and Christian could no more resist his words than he could resist the life Michel promised him.

As he headed down Fifth Avenue, the beauty of the snow glistening on the sidewalks reflected off his white skin. He could not help but wonder what had come over him, playing such a foolish game with Amanda. Initiating more contact between them only made his job harder, yet he sensed that they were already here, lying in wait for her.

Which vampire would come this time? Would Gaétan volunteer? Christian could not imagine Solange letting him out of her bed long enough to come to New York City. There were so many nameless ones competing for the chance to woo her. There were so many young ones with no sense of propriety or honor; vampires who would kill a mortal for no reason other than the joy of it. Enticing Amanda was not protecting her. But the temptation to play such a stupid game was too much, and he could not help wondering if she had found the box of matches he had dropped in Ross's office. Would she put the pieces together and come after him?

God forgive me for hoping so.

Chapter Eight

AMANDA ENTERED THE tiny midtown apartment she shared with Bethany. She had decided to make a quick dinner of pasta and a salad, and then try to nap before hitting the club scene later. Bethany had agreed to accompany her to the Grey Wolf tonight rather than go out for a drink with her boyfriend Jeff. If Christian was there, Amanda promised herself she would find him.

She flipped on the television and ate dinner on the sofa while catching up on the news. Bethany would not be home until at least nine o'clock. It was the beginning of tax season, and already she was putting in fourteen hour days. Amanda loved their cozy apartment, filled with eclectic used furniture, lots of stereo equipment, and shelves of books.

Family photographs, old maps of Paris, botanical prints, and several framed posters featuring French exhibitions at the Metropolitan Museum of Art hung on the sea green walls. An antique black-and-green Oriental rug covered the hardwood floor. Potted plants occupied the floor space in front of the living room windows, and Bethany's exercise bike and free weights sat in one corner.

Amanda slipped off her high heels and rested her feet on the coffee table as she wolfed down dinner. She glanced down at the matchbox resting on the coffee table. She was sure Ross was hiding something from her. *Thank God for that old sixth sense again, Amanda.* Ever since childhood, the random thoughts of others flashed into her mind as if they were being broadcast, like radio waves. She had never told anyone except Bethany and Ryan about it. He had laughed in her face.

Only years later she found out that he had a similar ability to read information from thoughts or objects. She guessed that the fear of his gifts made her brother try to hide them, first with marijuana and then heroin.

Then there was Christian. The stranger she had been searching for ever since that horrible night in Central Park. She had been hoping to see him again, trying to find him when suddenly he appeared in her life. How did he and Ross know each other? Amanda did not believe in accidents. Things happened for a reason she always told herself, until Ryan's death. What purpose had been served by his death? The shock of it still haunted her. She often woke in the night in a cold sweat from dreams of fighting off the monster that had killed him.

Amanda's mind drifted back to the night in the tunnel when Christian had come toward her, his hypnotic gaze moving over her. He was much more handsome in person than she remembered him being the night in the park. She closed her eyes, leaned back on the couch, and flipped off the TV. She knew that this man would change her life forever. *How can I stay away from him now that I know where to find him?* She did not trust herself, a realization that scared her.

No man had ever captivated her or dominated her thoughts as Christian had over the past six months. His deep voice and dark eyes drew her in like a magnet. Amanda felt her hands tangled in all his hair as he held her close. While he ran his smooth hands over her body, he kissed her passionately and she felt herself weaken. It was as if she were drowning in her own emotions, her lust and need for him. Cold lips pressed against her throat and when he pierced her skin she was not afraid as her own blood trickled down her neck.

"Amanda?" Bethany sat beside her, rubbing her head. "Hey, are you okay? You were moaning."

Amanda woke suddenly in a pool of sweat. It took her a minute to realize she had fallen asleep on the couch.

"Yeah, I'm fine." She rolled over toward the light from the kitchen. "What time is it Beth?"

"Just nine o'clock. Time to get cleaned up and go man hunting." Bethany smiled.

"Do you still want to come with me?"

"Yeah, why not? I am dying to meet this guy. Sounds like quite the hero and besides, what are friends for?" Bethany smiled again and flipped her long auburn hair behind her ears. At 5'7", she towered over Amanda and was as light as Amanda was dark. They had been best friends since junior high school and had shared the same dream of moving into the city the day after graduating high school. Both had attended NYU, but while Amanda had pursued both an undergraduate and graduate degree in Art History, Bethany had chosen a career in finance.

Amanda stood up slowly. "I'd better get in the shower."

"What does one wear to a Goth club?" Bethany called behind her, running her hair through her wavy auburn hair.

"Lots of black, my friend," Amanda said with a sigh as she stumbled into the bathroom.

"Well, that was interesting." Amanda climbed out of the idling cab. They were across the street front of the Grey Wolf.

"I think he thought we were hookers." Bethany laughed as she slammed the cab door. The cab driver had not been able to take his eyes off them.

"Maybe it's the dress, or the lipstick." Amanda looked down at her stiletto black heals and wool coat that covered a short black satin dress. A white lace petticoat peeked out just below the hemline. It was the latest fashion, especially when paired with sparkling black stockings. It was not her usual tailored wear-to-the-museum style, but she felt sexy.

Will this get his attention?

She noticed her reflection in the cab's window. Bethany had convinced her to apply lipstick, something she rarely wore. The color was dark, but not trashy and ironically titled *Blood Lust*. It felt strangely appropriate for this evening. Also reflected in the cab's window was the red neon sign Grey Wolf, which loomed in the darkness on the two-story loft.

So this is the place. Amanda's heart was racing. *Suppose he is here, then what?*

Surrounded by trendy shops and restaurants, the club had become the most popular night spot in the West Village. On weekends, the line extended around the block, like a dark snake moving through the narrow streets. Tonight was no exception. It was Friday night and despite the snow, the club would be crowded.

As Amanda crossed Bleeker Street, the image of the one Christian had called Lucien filled her head. His dark, empty eyes suddenly morphed into Thomas's face. Amanda had forgotten to tell Bethany about her possible date with Thomas. As she recalled her fantasy of making love to Christian and surrendering her neck to him, a thought crossed her mind. *Suppose Ryan was right. What if they* are *all vampires?*

Chapter Nine

IT WAS ELEVEN o'clock, and already the club was full of mortals anxious for another night of drinking, dancing, and mingling with the undead. Christian sat at the main bar and watched Michel mix a chocolate martini for a young overweight blonde. He smiled and laughed with the young woman as she leaned closer, unable to take her eyes off him. Another bartender and vampire, his friend Sabin seemed more focused while he mixed drinks, barely smiling at the women at the bar. Even the snow had not kept them away tonight.

Christian questioned his affect on women. Watching Michel, he realized that it was more than just vampiric powers that held women in Michel's sway. Even as a young man in France, they had fallen all over him. He was charming and a good listener. Christian watched as his best friend simultaneously mixed drinks, talked with customers, and held a cell phone pressed to his ear. He effortlessly moved from one woman to another, each of whom hoped to catch his gaze.

Women in black leather and heavy eye makeup poured into the club. The smell of blood, perfume, sweat, and alcohol bombarded him. It was almost too much for his senses. Soon the upstairs would fill up as naïve mortals coiled around one another, hoping to rub shoulders with a real vampire. He had never relished the idea of being the center of attention or being a part of a circus act, and he avoided the young barflies as much as possible.

Multitudes of impressionable young men and women came to the Grey Wolf seeking out their kind, but few gained the honor of becoming a donor. Christian could think of other words for what they did with his friends, mingling sex and blood in the private rooms upstairs. He scanned the narrow entranceway as more women poured into the club. If they approached him, he simply scowled until they left him alone.

"Don't look so excited," Michel chuckled sarcastically approaching Christian. "Why did you bother coming tonight? No new novels to read?"

Christian shrugged. He tolerated the club just to hang out in the bar with his friend; astonished that after nearly three hundred years of friendship he never tired of Michel's company. Usually he was content just to sit there but tonight he was distracted, watching the crowd; waiting.

Aside from Michel and Sabin, Christian enjoyed the company of very few vampires and even fewer mortals; Detective Burt Ross was the exception. When he had come down to the Grey Wolf to investigate the homicide of a young barfly, most of the vampires had fled, fearing persecution. Ross had managed to make the investigation go away, earning Christian's trust, and to a lesser degree, Michel's. Christian knew that Ross was enamored of him and he liked the fact that there was no guesswork to Ross. The vampire admired his values and persona. He said what he meant, and he meant what he said. Compared to the shrouded world of his kind, where nothing was ever as it seemed and most vampires were not to be trusted, Christian found Ross's honesty refreshing and strangely comforting.

He was pulled out of his thoughts by Michel calling his name above the loud music, just as her scent hit him. Although it was too crowded to see her, Christian knew she had just entered the club.

"You look like you've seen a ghost, my friend. What is it?" Michel asked.

Amanda followed Bethany into a huge room with high ceilings. It took a minute to adjust to the darkness. Loud dance music blared from huge speakers suspended from a second-floor catwalk. They stood for a moment as young men and women moved past them. Amanda scanned the room, not exactly sure what she was looking for. The crowd was made up of mostly young, average-looking college students wearing way too much leather and eye makeup.

Pink and blue lights bathed them in an eerie glow as her gaze followed the catwalk around the second floor. The high ceiling blended into the shadows and a large bar filled up the center of the room. Off to the left of the bar was a dance floor filled with more men and women who looked liked Goth GQ models.

"This way," Bethany yelled, grabbing her hand. "If anyone knows their clientele, it's the bartender."

Amanda held her girlfriend's sweaty hand as they pushed their way through the crowds toward the bar. It was wall-to-wall people, and getting anywhere was slow work. Turning abruptly, Bethany backtracked toward the entrance and then made a sharp left. Amanda realized that she was circumventing the crowd by hugging the outside walls of the bar. She saw an opening, and they made another left, still pushing their way through the crowds.

It was then that Amanda spotted him leaning against the bar. He towered over the people around him. She recognized his brown leather coat from the precinct. He was talking to someone who was blocked from their view.

"I see him." Amanda yelled out to her. "Keep walking."

As if he sensed her presence, he stopped talking and looked right at her. Half his face was hidden behind a curtain of hair but their eyes locked as she came closer. It was then that she saw a dark-haired man behind the bar. He wore a short black bolero jacket open to his waist, exposing a white chest. He moved with unusual grace and speed for a man, pulling down glasses and mixing drinks while talking on his cell phone and flirting with women at the bar.

"That's Christian, isn't it?" Bethany yelled at Amanda.

Amanda took her friend's hand and pulled her closer to the bar.

Christian nodded, making room for the two women. "Ms. Perretti, what a coincidence."

The bartender came closer, dangling a wine glass by the stem.

"Michel, this is Amanda Perretti." Christian gestured as if he were presenting her.

Amanda felt Michel's eyes peer into her as if she were under his personal microscope, yet she could get no read on him. She felt as though she had smacked up against an invisible wall.

"Welcome to the Grey Wolf." He said, and she heard the trace of a French accent.

Then he kissed her hand before she could react.

Amanda could not believe her luck. "This is my best friend Bethany Daniels."

Bethany nodded, unable to take her eyes off both men.

"What is your pleasure this evening?" Michel's voice felt like silk wrapping around her. *He reminds me of Thomas in a weird way,* she thought. *Maybe it's the way his voice makes me feel.*

"I'll have a glass of Merlot, thanks." Bethany blurted out and reached for her purse.

"Nothing for me, thank you." Amanda waved her hand.

"It's on the house, my beauty." He smiled, poured and then pushed the wine glass toward Bethany.

Michel seemed young, with his smooth skin and flirtatious manner. In fact, they both looked young, yet their eyes spoke of age and pain. Christian's were especially bottomless, yet sensual, while Michel's seemed icy and cold under all his bravado. She sensed a deep connection between them.

Out of habit, Christian flipped his hair behind him. "So we meet again?"

"They say that meeting once is coincidence but meeting twice is fate." Michel winked at her.

"Is that what they say, Michel?" She smiled, staring at Christian. "This is quite the place. Do you come here often?"

"We own it." Michel blurted out before Christian could respond to her question.

Amanda was surprised at his candidness. She glanced at Bethany, who gave her one of her "are they both for real" looks.

"I was telling Bethany how I happened to meet you at the police station."

Michel leaned on the bar. "Well, it is the night for coincidences, I must say."

"I happened to be visiting detective Ross when Ms. Perretti arrived." Christian confessed.

Michel raised his eyebrows at him.

"Could I speak to you for a moment?" Amanda interrupted, "I just need a minute of your time, if you don't mind." Amanda felt herself blush under Christian's intense gaze.

Christian nodded at Michel and ushered her away from the bar. Amanda followed, trying to keep up with his strides as he led her up a flight of steps and onto the catwalk. Christian stopped abruptly in front of a glass wall. He pushed against it and a door opened inward. Christian held it as Amanda hesitantly stepped into a dimly lit room. A mahogany bar ran the length of the small room. Black lacquered tables and chairs were scattered throughout. A mirror ran the full length of the wall behind the bar.

"Have a seat." He gestured, walking toward a table. The rustling sound of his leather coat seemed loud in the empty room.

"The bar is fine."

Her high heels echoed on the black and white tiles as she passed him. She checked her appearance in the full-length mirror as he approached. He was silent and graceful for someone so tall. She tried not to stare as he stopped beside her.

She suddenly felt nervous as she fumbled around in her purse for the book of matches. Remembering they were in her coat pocket she tossed them on the bar.

"It's my lucky night. I have been looking for you since last July and I find these in the Detectives' office."

Amanda focused her attention on him. The color of his wavy hair reminded her of wheat viewed through filtered sunlight, and his brown eyes darted nervously, never resting on anything for long, except when he turned his gaze toward her. Amanda thought his features were chiseled yet delicate for a man's, but she didn't consider his beauty otherworldly like Michel. Despite his lean frame and flowing hair, he was utterly masculine and commanding.

Christian said nothing, but picked up the matchbook, a silver signet ring on his pinky finger, caught the light. It reminded her of a piece of man's jewelry she had researched for the recent exhibition on *Jewelry of the French Revolution.* Amanda wanted to ask him about it, but then thought better of it.

"Why don't you sit down?" He gestured toward a bar stool.

"I'll stand, thank you. Do you work here, too?"

"I am a rare book dealer."

"Really? You impress me as more of the musician type. Where is your shop?"

"I work from my home." He tossed the matchbook onto the bar.

"I tried to catch up with you at the precinct," she began, unsure of where to start. "I can't believe I finally ran into you after all these months. You have to understand, I am still trying to make sense of what happened that night in Central Park. I—"

"Amanda, I can assure you. You have the wrong man." He touched her hand gently and she felt her knees buckle as what felt like an electric current ran up her arm.

"There cannot be two men who look like you."

He smiled slightly and Amanda noticed his beautiful white teeth. His smile seemed to transform his face, and for a moment he seemed to relax.

She smiled back at him in the mirror. He was too beautiful to stare at directly.

"I am not looking to involve the police. I just need some answers. I know I sound crazy but—"

"I am sorry you had to come all the way down here."

She gently touched his arm. He felt cold.

"Ryan was saying such strange things the night that he was murdered. He was talking about a club, hanging out with these people who were beautiful and different. And in the same breath he was talking about—"

She caught her reflection in the mirror. *I can't believe I am going to say this aloud.*

"Amanda, your brother sounds like a very troubled soul," Christian interrupted. He pushed the matchbook down the bar towards her. "Why don't you go home and try to move past such an unfortunate turn of events."

He stepped back as if he were dismissing her but she ignored him. "He was talking about selling his blood to vampires. I know it sounds bizarre, but I know my brother, Christian. He was addicted to heroin, but he was not crazy."

"Vampires," he whispered, shaking his head. "You don't believe in that nonsense, do you?"

"I'm not so sure anymore. Look, I may work in a museum surrounded by all this physical stuff, but I consider myself to be a very open-minded person. I am not above believing Ryan came into contact with someone or something . . . unusual."

"And the possibility of that does not frighten you?"

"I'm not sure," she confessed, shaking her head. "It sounds farfetched and crazy, but I think the man that attacked him was a vampire. I did a little research, and one of the ways to kill a vampire is through decapitation."

He chuckled halfheartedly.

"You laugh, but my brother's blood poured onto the pavement right before my eyes." She stared off into space as if reliving that night. "This thing was covered in his blood....I still lose sleep over it."

"Any self-respecting vampire would never allow that to happen." Christian waved his hand dramatically, coming closer. "An immortal would have hypnotized him first. The effect is like being pulled into a dark chasm that has no return, and yet you go there willingly. If your brother had been a woman, the vampire would have kissed her gently with cold lips before sinking his fangs into her warm flesh. She would have no sense of her life being drained away by the beautiful specter until it was too late."

Amanda listened to his deep, soothing voice. The experience he described was terrifying, and yet so inviting and erotic that it made her blush, like her dream. She had no recollection of moving closer to him, but suddenly she was next to him, being pulled into his eyes. His leather coat rubbed against her stockings and she realized that she was wedged between the bar stool and his body.

She froze, unable to break his gaze.

"You speak as if you are—"

"You need to leave now." He whispered. "We have spoken long enough of such things."

The pull of his dark eyes made her feel dizzy and she grabbed his coat for balance. *I can't let him leave now.* She searched his face for answers, yet found his eyes suddenly bottomless and cold. How could he be both inviting and perilous?

"Please, Christian, I—"

"I will not talk with you again, Ms. Perretti."

He was suddenly standing at the end of the bar.

"Just tell me you were there that night. God damn it, be honest with me."

"I will not ask you again to leave!"

She tried not to shake as she paused at the door, angry at being dismissed by the very man who intrigued her.

"Fine, I'll go. But this isn't over between you and me. Not by a long shot."

The loud music slammed against her as she rushed back down the hallway, dodging people on the stairs. She hoped Bethany was still waiting for her at the bar yet dreaded having to meet up with her there. She wanted just to duck out into the cold night and go home.

How could I have let this go so poorly?

In the soft light of the side bar, Christian felt himself losing control over the young woman he was sworn to protect. He fought the pull of her beauty and his very nature, a nature born of power and lust filtered through the constant need for blood. He wanted to both shield her from harm and bury his fangs in her beautiful neck. He had fought hard to master control of his vampire nature, to be more than a parasite with a beautiful face who could take what he wanted with no rules or laws to govern him. It had been a hard fight that had cost him much, and here before him was the fruit of his self-restraint and his self-control. *She is not afraid of me. She questions whether we are blood drinkers, intrigued by the idea of surrender.*

He had studied her face in the mirror, the tilt of her eyes, the curve of her lips and her high cheekbones framing thick wild hair. Her skin had a warm brown glow as if she had spent the day at the beach. Her hands were long and narrow and he noticed that she chewed her fingernails. She was quiet yet direct, feminine yet strong-willed. Her attire made his blood boil, embarrassed by the thoughts racing through his head. He thought she looked good next to him.

If only it could have been different.

Christian put his face in his hands and closed his eyes, willing himself back from the rage that threatened to consume him. For a moment, he thought about catching up to her and bringing her back. She could not have gotten too far. He could sit her down, and explain how the present intersection of their lives had been forged over two hundred years ago with the birth of his daughter, Solange Du Mauré; the child of a mortal woman and a vampire.

Yes, she'll buy that one, he thought. *Then I'll tell her I am a vampire, that vampire.* He tried, but he could not squelch his fury. It was born of rage and fueled by guilt over hating his only daughter, the bringer of so much pain and suffering to his life.

He picked up a glass ashtray and threw it at his reflection. The ashtray shattered against the back bar, like falling snow.

Chapter Ten

❧

CHRISTIAN CURLED UP in the large leather chair in the office of the Grey Wolf. He so hated grand displays of emotion and tonight had rattled him. Distracted, he took apart a paper clip, while the music of Beethoven played in the background in an attempt to calm his frazzled nerves.

The walls, floor, and the ceiling of the small office were lacquered black, giving the room a cold, cave-like feel. A glass-topped desk filled up the far right corner of the room, a hint of Michel's preference for modern decor. A gray leather couch faced the desk on the opposite wall. Behind the couch, a framed black and white poster held the image of a lost-looking Humphrey Bogart. The word *Casablanca* scrawled across the top of the poster. Christian knew it was Michel's favorite movie and had made a concession.

On the far left wall were two framed lithographs. The first was an 1870 map of Central Park. The second was the Bois du Boulogne in Paris, dating from 1790. Both were lit, giving the room the feel of a library. They were the only hint of Christian's influence in the office. Below the maps stood a tall bookcase overflowing with CDs of numerous musical styles, a small stereo system, and a portable TV. The bookcase was Plexiglas, so the objects appeared to float in space.

Hung on a door at the far end of the room was a color poster of the Rolling Stones, circa 1972. The door led to a bedroom that Michel used frequently for the seducing of the young women who came to the club. The instinct for self-preservation demanded they keep their Upper East Side townhouse private, away from the prying eyes of mortals. Tony, a male barfly, lived with them and handled the daily activities required to retain an air of normalcy for the two vampires.

Michel gently closed the office door behind him. "How did she find you?"

Christian had never lied to Michel, but he could not admit to himself why he had lured her here.

Michel went to sit down. "I never realized how beautiful—"

Christian grabbed his best friend. They had shared many women between them, but his stomach twisted in a knot at Michel's words. What would it mean if he tried to take the young mortal away from him?

"Don't even think about touching her, Michel." Christian could barely force the words out.

"I meant no harm, my friend." Michel raised his hands in surrender.

"My job is to protect her, though I am not sure how to anymore."

Michel sat down on the edge of the desk. "What did you say to her? She looked frazzled yet determined when she left, and I imagine she will keep coming back until you thoroughly convince her you are not the madman who beheaded her brother's murderer and saved her life."

Michel was joking, but Christian was not in a jovial mood. He had tried to hypnotize her that night yet she had described everything, including Christian, in disturbing detail. Ross had shown him the police report. She was more powerful than he had anticipated; more powerful than Ryan.

"She handed me this before she left." Michel reached into his pocket for the envelope.

Christian stared at it as if it were on fire, hesitating to touch it.

"Aren't you going to read it?" Michel shoved the note into Christian's hand. He tore open the envelope.

Dear Christian,
We need to talk. I am not afraid of you. Please call me at 555-232-7717
or come by the museum any time.

Amanda

Frustrated, he tore up the note and tossed the pieces into the air. *Sure, and we'll do lunch too.*

The paper shreds floated to the floor like snow and reminded him of his choices, both the night he followed Michel into darkness and now, as his long-ago promise to Josette haunted him.

"What does she want?" Michel impulsively began to pick up the pieces of paper.

"What I cannot give her: the truth." He began to twist a strand of his long hair around his finger, a habit born in his youth.

"Why won't you just talk with her?" Michel looked up from the floor, still scooping up pieces of the note.

"And tell her what, Michel? I broke my own rules and interfered. In trying to protect them both, I failed, and now he's dead and she is in mortal danger. Christ, I wouldn't even turn Solange when I found out she was dying."

"Stop torturing yourself, Christian. You have watched over them all in homage to Josette, but who knows, Amanda may be the last of them."

Michel's declaration twisted a knot in Christian's stomach as he realized that something could happen to her, and then what would he do? His entire existence had been devoted to Josette and the descendants of his daughter, Solange. London. California. New York. All because of them. He had never allowed himself to consider Amanda's premature death, but he could not imagine her future as a wife and mother. In his mind's eye she was forever young and beautiful, existing only for him.

"I made a promise to Josette, Michel. I suppose that would mean nothing to you."

"Let it be over, Christian." Michel got up and dusted off his knees. "Their attack is inevitable, so turn her or kill her."

Christian grabbed him by his jacket. "Are you worried? Let them try to slaughter us."

"It is not me that I worry about." Michel brushed a strand of hair away from Christian's face. "You have become obsessed with her."

"I have an obligation to Josette, or have you forgotten?"

"It is you who have forgotten that we have the power to turn her. Then she would stand a fighting chance."

"Are you out of your mind, Michel?"

"Don't tell me that you haven't thought about taking some of her precious blood for yourself?"

"I would rather kill her first," Christian hissed, reaching for his coat.

"You may just have to, because the way I see it, there are few options here," Michel snapped back as Christian slammed the door.

Christian left the Grey Wolf and headed toward Seventh Avenue. He touched the leather strap at his chest for reassurance. Michel had suggested he take Amanda's blood for himself, but the thought of ever taking advantage of her was inconceivable. Michel could no more imagine being responsible for anyone other than himself than Christian could imagine abandoning Amanda now.

How dare Michel perceive his need to protect her as something sordid and lustful! That was the way he viewed women, objects to be seduced and discarded and just because his life had been filled with sex and blood alone, Christian could not condone it. It was where they differed and yet Michel had followed Christian from Paris to London, and then to the New World. He loved Paris and could have easily stayed back, but he had come along. Still, Michel had always been a *roué* and that was not about to change now.

He walked faster, trying to clear his head. Let Michel stay behind at the club with all those mortals. Michel had always loved being amongst them. He found comfort and life's meaning in their world. Christian could never understand his continual fascination with them. He thought Michel would outgrow it, but he never did, and Christian had given up trying to convince his best friend otherwise. He headed up Seventh Avenue through Washington Square Park. The temperature was dropping, and a thin blanket of snow covered the sidewalks.

Maybe Ross was around, or he could sneak into the Metropolitan Museum of Art. He loved to walk around the museum alone at night, something he had done since coming to New York in 1901. Art was his passion, and although he sometimes walked the halls of the Met amongst mortals, he delighted in sneaking past the guards and the security cameras. Being cold-blooded, he could not set off the heat sensors in the galleries. Though he would never see the masterpieces in the daylight, he still treasured these visits.

He took secret pleasure in knowing this was Amanda's sanctuary, the place she spent most of her days and many a Friday night. He knew of her passion for eighteenth-century France. When he found himself there one Saturday night, wandering the galleries in the hopes of seeing her in person, he knew he was getting too involved in her life. Saturday night was date night at the Met. Couples floated through the dimly lit galleries, holding hands and gazing at the priceless art.

One night he saw her there with a well-dressed older man whose manner seemed distant; a frown marred his otherwise handsome features. Christian sensed a deeper connection between them.

A lover perhaps?

Amanda looked dazzling, in a low-cut, long black dress with a triple strand of pearls. He stood a safe distance and watched them at a table for two, listening to Chamber music, drinking wine by candlelight.

How romantic, he thought, although they barely spoke to one another. He imagined himself sitting with her, talking and laughing, yet this man said little. He seemed bored. Christian was surprised at the jealousy he felt well up within him as he spied on them.

When they left the museum he followed them back to an apartment on the Upper East Side, not too far from his townhouse. He lingered outside the building and imagined being alone with her, slipping her out of her elegant, black dress, running his lips along her warm neck, past the pearls—

His ringing cell phone jarred him out of his fantasy. He knew who it was before he opened his phone.

"Hello, Ross." He looked both ways before crossing 14th Street and headed north on Sixth Avenue. "Don't you ever sleep?" Christian asked, hearing the familiar sound of Ross exhaling a cigarette.

"I'm a cop, for Christ's sake."

"And I'm a vampire, but I probably get more sleep than you."

"We need to finish our conversation. Can you meet me now?"

"I'm on my way." The vampire snapped his cell phone shut. The temperature had fallen, and the layers of snow coating the sidewalks had turned to ice. Most people took cabs or public transportation this time of year, leaving the sidewalks empty and the streets congested and noisy. Christian cut across Broadway and continued uptown toward the Museum of Modern Art. He stuck to the side streets rather than the avenues. He hated getting his hair windblown.

He had known by the look on Ross's face earlier that something was on his mind, but then Amanda had shown up, startling them both. His emotions were getting the better of him and he hated himself for it. The machete against his back reminded him of their plight. When he glanced at his reflection, he reminded himself of a dark angel with his leather coat flowing out behind him; sword strapped to his back.

Chapter Eleven

THE MANHATTAN CLUB sat on the corner of West 57th and Broadway. The luxury hotel had a beautiful after-hours club that reminded Christian of the Oak Room in the historic Plaza Hotel.

As Christian approached it seemed that the condensation on the front windows made the patrons inside appear to be no more than colored shadows, barely visible through the glass. As he stepped inside the dimly lit bar, their conversations buzzed in his head. He could smell Ross already here, in his usual spot away from the crowd.

A balding, middle aged maître d' greeted him with barely any eye contact before turning on his heels. Christian followed him past the overstuffed couches and potted palms toward the back of the large room. He made a sharp right toward a private corner, stopping just short of an occupied couch.

This was their usual spot, away from the prying eyes and ears of the masses who could not take their eyes off the stunning vampire. Ross's usual martini sat on the coffee table. Christian took a seat on the green velvet couch opposite him. He tried to lean back against the couch, but the sharp machete forced him to sit upright.

"Why don't you take it off and make yourself comfortable?" Ross smiled and took a sip of his drink.

Christian slipped off his leather coat and tossed it on the couch next to him. He scanned the room and then, in a motion Ross could not follow, slid the threatening blade from behind his back and shoved it under the couch cushion. He adjusted his shirt just as the familiar waiter approached

"The usual?" He asked, giving the vampire a weak smile.

"Please." Christian nodded. Although he could no longer eat or drink, he had never lost his love of Cognac. Prior to tonight, it had been months since he had spoken with the detective. He set his cell phone on the dark wood table next to Ross's.

After the waiter left, Christian lifted the glass in a toast, as Ross raised his as well. Then the vampire set it back down on the table. Crossing one leg over his other knee, Christian sat back against the couch. The soft velvet felt good against his skin, and the darkness soothed him. As far as a mortal hangout went, the Manhattan Club was alright.

Ross swallowed the last of his martini.

"If you see the waiter, flag him down, okay?"

"I'll do better than that, Ross. I'll plant the seed." Christian telepathically connected with the waiter and suggested he bring another drink.

"Man." Ross chuckled after the waiter had deposited a second martini, "If I had your gifts, I would be getting more ass than a toilet seat."

"Wrong vampire," Christian smirked, referring to Michel. Christian had fantasized about taking blood from Ross, but he was a friend. A friend he knew would bend his neck without thinking twice about it. Michel was the only male Christian ever took blood from; the act was so intimate that he could not imagine crossing that line with another man.

"You lucky bastards." Ross grinned, shaking his head as he picked up his drink and met the vampire's brown eyes. Christian knew Ross was intrigued and was always trying to imagine what life must truly be like for a vampire. Handling the investigation at the Grey Wolf early last summer had given him an up close and personal look at their lifestyle. Ross had mentioned to Christian that he likened it to being a famous celebrity, glamorous and exciting at first, then alarming and disturbing in the long run. Christian liked the analogy. Christian impulsively sniffed his drink, waiting for Ross to tell him the real reason for his call

"Speaking of luck, imagine, running right into Amanda Perretti tonight? How is that for a coincidence?" Ross smiled.

"Yes, it was quite the twist of fate."

"Twist of fate, man. I could feel the vibes between you both. I thought you said you could hypnotize humans."

Christian shrugged, flipping his hair behind him. Yes, there *were* vibes between them, and it terrified him.

"She always stuck to her story of seeing you in the park. Hey, you can't blame the girl for wanting to see you up close and personal." He began to stir his martini.

"Now, I need you to tell me the real reason we're here, Ross."

Ross put the martini glass down and leaned closer.

"Every winter we find homeless people frozen to death in the park. It happens, you know? We try to round 'em all up when it gets really cold, but sometimes we miss a few."

He took a sip of his martini.

"Anyway, about a week ago I was reviewing a list of case files from the past six months with one of the other shift officers. It's standard procedure kind of stuff, but I noticed that certain case files are still open, which means there is an ongoing murder investigation. When I questioned Briggs, he explained that these victims were found in the park . . . and that someone thought maybe they hadn't frozen to death after all."

Christian leaned closer; he tried to pick up the detective's thoughts but Ross was one of those rare mortals he could not read. Whenever he tried he got static, like turning a radio dial too quickly. Ross's thoughts were jumbled and incoherent to Christian.

"How many people are we talking about, Ross?"

Ross swallowed an olive. "Enough to suggest a pattern."

Christian's dark stare compelled him to keep talking.

"The rate of decomposition indicates the presence of maggots inside the body. Maggots feed off tissue, using the body cavity for warmth. When we tried to thaw the bodies, they basically caved in on themselves due to the lack of a solid infrastructure." Ross made a crushing gesture with his hands.

"I don't follow you."

"There was massive blood loss yet no apparent fatal wound. These victims probably died last fall and were left in the park, so their decomposed remains froze."

"But you just said that these were homeless people who had no money or other valuables. What could they possibly have that anyone would want to kill them for?"

Christian flashed back to his early days in Paris when he and Michel had been young vampires just learning how to master their craving for blood. Poverty and disease had left thousands of children orphaned and abandoned in the city, and they had survived on them. He and Michel had stayed especially close to hospitals. From there they could whisk ailing children away in the night. They were going to die anyway, Gabrielle had reminded them, and no one would miss them. Christian had hated her for being right, yet hunting the weak and the sick had soothed his conscience back then, making the slaughter easier. He knew vampires who killed for the mere sport of it, just because they had the power. Like Gaétan, Gabrielle, or Solange. But he was not one of them.

A sudden chill brought him back to the present.

"They were drained of their blood, weren't they?" Christian asked, trying to speak softly.

"We found little in any of the bodies."

"Are you suggesting this is another Diane Reese situation?"

Christian could hear Ross's heart rate accelerating and could smell fear on him.

"I am not suggesting anything, Christian, just giving you the facts."

Christian could still see her; contorted, naked and drained of all blood, lying in a dumpster behind the Grey Wolf. A tall blonde; nothing special. Ross said she had a history of drug abuse and no family to speak of. Her name was Diane Reese and she had joined the ranks of the disposable ones and become another statistic. Ross had been able to connect her murder to a psychotic homeless man who had been terrorizing women in the area, instead of to an inexperienced young vampire.

"Where in the park were they found?" Christian whispered, afraid of the answer.

"Mostly in the ravine section. You know, it's so remote up there that we don't patrol it daily like we do the more populated areas of the park."

Christian leaned so close to the detective he could smell his deodorant. "You know that my kind have been hunting in the park since I came here at the turn of the century. Most vampires will do anything in their power to remain anonymous and unknown. We have a very strong self-preservation streak. This is not good news."

"Well, whoever is doing this obviously either doesn't know the rules or doesn't give a shit about getting caught. Anyone you know from out of town that might be—"

Christian was up before Ross could finish his sentence. He slipped the machete back into place and had his coat on before Ross could say another word.

"What is it?" Ross asked, trying to stop the vampire from slipping past him.

"I hope my instincts are wrong. I'll call you."

Then the vampire was gone, leaving Ross alone with his martini and the check.

After calling Michel to relate his conversation with Ross, Christian combed the entire park. He was looking for something unusual—a smell or a feeling from one of the old ones—but he sensed nothing out of the ordinary. Once in the ravine, a private and rustic section of the park, he took out his machete. Since the elevation was below the regular grade of the park, the skyline was lost from view making the paths harder to navigate for the average mortal. Christian had no trouble following the pathways that had no street lamps, and his keen ears could hear the babbling loch up ahead, not yet frozen.

He suddenly sensed something up ahead: an energy that belonged to only one being; a vampire. Looking closely, he saw him on the wooden bridge, silhouetted by two giant red oak trees. He sensed curiosity more than anything else from the other immortal, but held on to his machete nonetheless. Christian knew most of the other vampires in the city, but he usually chose to keep his distance from them.

"Christian, is that you?" A high-pitched male voice with a British accent called out in the darkness.

"Peter?" The vampire lowered his machete and moved closer. The spark from a cigarette lighter illuminated a plain face with shaggy brown hair and dull blue eyes. In a down coat, blue jeans, and sneakers, Peter looked more like a tourist than a vampire. Christian put the machete back in its sling.

"Jesus Christ, I hope you weren't planning to use that on me?" He exhaled, shoving the cigarettes back in his coat pocket.

"What are you doing here?"

"I might ask you the same thing Christian. Walking around the ravine waving your weapon seems just a little foreboding, wouldn't you say?" He exhaled quickly.

Christian and Michel had met Peter in the 1960s. He had been a mortal from Britain who came to America for a rock festival. He had met up with a roadie vampire at Woodstock who changed his life forever. He was harmless, but Christian could not help but wonder what he was doing here. He stopped just shy of the center of the bridge, giving Peter space, a sign of respect and no harm intended.

"I suppose so. I haven't seen you since last fall. Michel and I thought you might have gone back across the pond."

"How is Michel these days, still gorgeous beyond belief?"

Christian shrugged. "Some things never change."

Peter began pacing. Christian had always known him to be restless. In fact, he seemed to have adopted more human qualities than vampire traits, even more so than Michel. His pacing and smoking reminded Christian of Ross or any other high-strung New Yorker living in such a stressful age.

"How are things, Peter? You seem a bit agitated tonight."

Christian came closer and leaned against the carved wooden railing on the bridge. The sound of the water running under the bridge soothed him.

"I don't know," the other vampire said with a shrug. "I just came back tonight to have a look around. I've been hanging out in Battery Park since this bloke showed up here. Gave me the creeps, he did—"

"Was he a vampire or just your typical New York psycho?"

Peter stamped out his cigarette then lit another one. "He's one of us, but as soon as I saw him I knew something wasn't right about him. I said to myself, 'Peter, this bastard would cut out your heart and shit in the hole if it pleased him.' Then some of the old-timers here started disappearing—"

"Mortals?" Christian asked, sniffing the darkness but sensing no other presence there.

"Yeah, I mean some of those people lived here for a long time. I'd take a sip from them on occasion, usually when I couldn't find a man to my liking." He chuckled, confirming for Christian that Peter was indeed gay. Michel believed Peter was always after him.

"I asked Willy, one of the locals who I've gotten to know, and he told me that this guy approached them all sweet and nice, offering them money for sex, and then . . ." Peter ran two fingers across his throat in the sign of execution.

"What did he look like?"

"Willy said he was average height like me, not tall and handsome like you and Michel." He eyed Christian up and down. "His hair was brown and longish, but his eyes were black and empty-looking, even in the sunlight. I heard he had an accent like yours—"

"So he's French?"

"Oui, oui," Peter chuckled again, taking a drag from his cigarette. "I believe so. They said he was boyishly cute, actually."

"I never heard a vampire described as cute, Peter—"

"Well, apparently he has dimples and quite the smile."

"Maybe I can speak to this Willy character myself?" Christian thought he could push into his mind and get more information, though the picture was starting to become clear.

"He's dead, Christian. In fact, a lot of them are dead now. Thomas killed them all." He stamped out his second cigarette.

"Thomas?"

Peter shrugged and pulled another cigarette out of his pack, then shoved the pack back into his coat pocket.

"That's what he called himself."

Christian made Peter promise that if the stranger showed up again he would contact either Christian or Michel at the Grey Wolf. He also gave him their cell phone numbers just in case. Christian had just stepped off the rugged bridge, replaying their conversation in his head when something Peter had said suddenly hit him.

He caught up with the other vampire just on the other side of the loch.

"This Thomas character, did you ever run across him here in the park?"

"Well actually, I've never met him myself."

Peter had a deer in the headlights look on his youthful face.

"Peter, you said something back there. Something about his eyes looking black and empty, even in the sunlight?"

"That's just it, Christian. It was broad daylight when Willy met up with Thomas."

The look on Christian's face confirmed the fear in Peter's eyes.

"That's right, my friend. This one's both a night and a day walker."

PART THREE

Chapter Twelve

AMANDA TRIED NOT to appear annoyed when Thomas's cell phone vibrated again. He tried to ignore it and concentrate on their conversation but Amanda knew he was distracted. Zero Hour was a far cry from the Grey Wolf. A huge Maplewood bar took up the center of the room and three of the four walls were mirrored, giving the impression the club was much larger than it appeared. Low lighting and jazz music gave it a romantic feel and Amanda felt more comfortable in a black turtleneck, black trousers, and little jewelry.

After the disaster at the Grey Wolf, she thought she might have better luck with Thomas, and besides, she could not spend another Saturday night at home. She had put up a strong front for Bethany, but as she lay in bed she cried at the thought that Christian had rejected her, promising never to talk to her again. At least that's how it felt to her. So, at the last minute she had decided to take a chance on Thomas.

"Amanda, you have to excuse me a moment." He leaned in close. "I have to take this call."

She sensed the caller was a woman; someone far away with dark hair and eyes, wearing a beautiful long black dress with unusual high heels. She had just assumed he was single, but maybe he had a wife or a steady girlfriend back in Paris. She realized that she knew very little about him. Their relationship was framed by their work at the museum and their love of eighteenth-century France. Outside of that, they were strangers. Amanda glanced around the room and sipped her wine. She wondered if coming here had been a good idea. Being here was an admission of feelings for him, something she had been surer of before meeting Christian last night.

Boy I blew that one. I finally meet the one man I have been dreaming about for the last six months and I manage to get thrown out of his club, all in the space of about ten minutes. Amanda had replayed their brief conversation on and off all day, especially the part where he described seducing someone to drink their blood. *The effect is like being pulled into a dark chasm that has no return yet you go willingly.*

Though she was having trouble believing he was a vampire *or* a rare book dealer, she understood what he was saying about being seduced by something that was potentially dangerous or life-threatening. In a strange way, her brother's murder had taken control of her life. It was as horrific as it was beguiling, and now she had met one of the cast of characters: Christian. Although he seemed staid and polite, he was dark and alluring as well. She felt drawn to him like a magnet.

Something made her turn around as if Christian were nearby. She scanned the crowd but saw only Thomas approaching her.

"Sorry about that." He appeared sheepish as he sat down.

"So, she wants to know when you're coming home, huh?"

He could not make eye contact with her.

"Thomas, you aren't married, are you? I don't—"

He smiled at her and she suddenly noticed how beautiful he was in the dim light of the bar.

"Would that make a difference?" He pulled her closer.

"The woman who has been calling you . . . ?"

He shrugged and brushed a strand of hair out of her face. "A girlfriend from back home. She misses me terribly."

Amanda searched his eyes, not sure if he was telling the truth.

Amanda smiled. "And do you miss her?"

"It's only you and me tonight." Something about the way he said it made her heart speed up, and suddenly she was kissing him. Never one for public displays of affection, she melted as he pulled her closer.

His breath felt warm against her ear. "Let me prove it to you Amanda."

She searched his eyes and found only desire there.

"Let me go to the bathroom, okay?" She smiled and grabbed her purse. "I'll be right back."

"I'll get a cab." He gestured towards the door. "Meet me out front."

She followed a group of women heading down the black carpeted steps to the bathrooms. At the bottom of the stairs, Amanda noticed private rooms off the hallway leading toward the bathrooms. Conscious of someone waiting for her, she made record time in the spacious ladies' room. She was headed back down the hallway when her cell phone buzzed.

Still unsure of whether she should go home with Thomas, she paused to read a text message from Bethany, who was sitting in a movie theatre with her boyfriend, Jeff. He had dragged her to a horror film that she hated, so she had decided to check in on her best friend.

Amanda followed the flow of traffic while she texted Bethany back and explained that she was leaving the club with Thomas.

"Sorry," she mumbled, walking right into someone as she continued to text.

"Amanda?"

She looked up into a pair of familiar dark eyes surrounded by flowing blond hair. He wore a ripped and tattered long-sleeved white shirt, and a pair of black jeans. Amanda felt her heart skip a beat. The woman beside him was almost as tall, with long, flowing dark hair that she had parted on the side; her black strapless dress contrasted against her white skin perfectly.

She tried not to stare at the beautiful woman as she forced a smile and dropped her phone in her purse.

"What a surprise. Hello Christian."

She could feel herself blushing. The woman wrapped her arm in his as if to say, "He's mine," and Amanda guessed that they were lovers. She was as beautiful as he was handsome.

Christian kept his gaze on Amanda, and she wished she had just left the bar with Thomas. *Oh, shit, Thomas.*

"Eve, this is Amanda."

Amanda nodded, faking a smile while Eve looked through her. She had to get away.

"Someone is waiting out front for me. I'd better run."

Before he could utter another word, she had rushed past them into the crowd.

She made her way upstairs, fighting tears and wondering if indeed he had been upstairs in the bar and it had not been her imagination. Thomas was standing against the building when she emerged. He had been on the phone, but closed it when she approached.

"Is everything okay?"

"Fine," she lied, feeling like a fool for thinking that Christian might be single.

How could a man like that not be taken? As they rode back to her place in the cab, she told herself it was for the best. *Everything happens for a reason.*

Eve opened her apartment door and let Christian in ahead of her. It had been months since he had been here. She gestured him into the modern living room of her twentieth-floor apartment overlooking Battery Park. Christian went to the wall of glass windows and stared out at the Statue of Liberty in the harbor. He felt her cold arms wrap around his waist.

"I'm not sure which is more upsetting," she whispered, grinding up against him. "Seeing how you looked at that little mortal, or the sense I get that you would rather be anywhere else than here with me."

Her voice still held traces of a southern drawl she had never lost. The widow of a Confederate general, Eve Beaumont had come to New York after the Civil War, looking for another husband but she had met another fate.

Christian had met her shortly after coming to New York, and although outwardly genteel, she was tough and Christian could use all the allies he could get right now. Still, Eve was right. He was just going through the motions with her. He had followed Amanda to Zero Hour and now she was with her boyfriend, somewhere out of reach.

"Come to bed with me," she whispered into his hair. "Let me take your mind off her, at least for a few hours."

Amanda's breath rose softly as she slept, her face illuminated by the incoming street light. It had been so long since he had made love to a mortal woman. The experience reminded him of being with Josette, and the brief happiness he had shared with her before Christian had stolen her away. Her bedroom smelled of sex and sweat, cocooning them both. He had about four hours until the sun rose as the effects of Ryan's blood were slowly beginning to wear off.

It had been six months since he had arrived in New York—the blink of an eye for the vampire, but Solange had begun calling him lately, asking if the mortal were dead, whether he had seen her father, and when would he be coming home? Thomas had few answers for her, and even fewer for himself. He no longer cared for or missed her. She was a spoiled, self-centered child who he had only turned in seeking revenge against Christian. Gabrielle's warning echoed in his head. *You turned her out of revenge and not love. No good will ever come of it.* What he had thought were the jealous ravings of a scorned woman had turned out to be a prophecy. He could no longer stomach the thought of Solange's embrace.

Her beauty was intoxicating and her lovemaking beyond any man's desires, but her narcissism diminished her power to captivate him. *Is spending so much time around these mortals influencing me?* He crawled back into bed beside Amanda and slowly ran his hand down her back. Her tan skin was warm to his touch. She mumbled something in her sleep and turned toward him. He instinctively pulled the covers around her to keep her warm. He was not sure when she had shifted from the unsuspecting pawn he met up with in the cafeteria to a mortal he cared about and did not want to harm, but it had happened and now he was unsure of himself.

Perhaps I can just forget about all of this and just go back to being Thomas, a night shift guard. But I cannot do it without the blood. I have almost none left. I could take just a little from her. She won't even remember it in the morning. Just a taste.

Amanda rolled over and noticed flowers and a note on her night stand. She heard the shower water running. It was eleven o'clock already.

Was he really here last night? What day is it?

Then she played back meeting him at the Zero Hour. She had never seen him out of uniform, and something about his tight black jeans and exotic shirt had made her blood boil. Their one drink had turned into two and before she knew it they were in a cab heading toward her place. It all seemed to happen so fast. He was a gentle yet experienced lover, with a touch that drove her mad, yet all the while she could not stop thinking about Christian and the beautiful woman with him.

The bouquet was something he had to have picked up at the corner market this morning. She stepped over her clothes strewn on the floor from the night before and grabbed a pair of boxer shorts and a T-shirt out of her dresser drawer.

Did I really spend the night with him?

Bethany's bedroom door was open, her overnight bag tossed on her bed. Her usual MO after spending the night at Jeff's place.

"Beth," she yelled, knocking on the bathroom door. "Are you in there?"

"What's up?" A muffled voice yelled back. "Come on in."

Amanda opened the door and was hit with steam and the smell of lavender. "What time did you get in?"

"About ten minutes ago, why?" Bethany yelled over the running water.

"I just thought maybe you had passed Thomas on your way in."

Bethany poked her head out from behind the shower curtain. "Thomas was here? You spent the night with him?"

"Yeah." She smiled hesitantly. "I even got flowers. I'll make some coffee."

She shut the door to Bethany's hoots and hollers. Ever since the night she had come over to the museum to meet Amanda after work and had met Thomas Bretagne, Bethany had been enamored of him and wondered why her best friend was not dating him. After the fiasco at the Grey Wolf the night before, Bethany had been less sympathetic about Amanda's interest in Christian. Zero Hour, she explained, was a normal upscale bar and Thomas seemed like a normal, likeable guy. Her advice to Amanda was clear; focus on Thomas and let Christian go.

Amanda opened the envelope with her name scrawled across the front, doubting her judgment and the vividness of her dream.

Amanda,

Last night was magic. Had to run, see you tomorrow.

Thomas

She absentmindedly rubbed her neck and felt something. She needed a hot shower, a hotter cup of coffee, and time to sort through last night. She tossed her clothes into the hamper and straightened up her bed. *What the hell?*

There was a dark stain on her pillow. She wet her finger and touched the stain, then licked her fingertips. The liquid tasted bitter and coppery.

Blood.

Christian left Eve's apartment and headed home before dawn. The city was finally quiet, and he decided to walk uptown to clear his head. Eve had promised to keep an ear out for any foreign vampires in her part of the city, but the price was her possessiveness. As long as he was willing to make love to her and share blood, she would do whatever he asked. Eve was beautiful, like Gabrielle, but she had no desire for power. She was still an old fashioned woman who wanted wealth and a man to control both it and her.

She was sensual, but shallow, with a love of fine jewels and expensive clothing. He thought she and Michel would have made a perfect match, but ironically they could not stand each other. Christian attributed it to the phenomena of seeing the exact character traits you possess in someone else and hating them for it.

He wondered where Amanda had raced off to at Zero Hour, and with whom. He decided to duck into the museum as he approached it. He entered through the freight entrance on 82nd Street. As he headed north through a labyrinth of hallways, he scoured the offices and studios that housed the less glamorous but equally integral parts of the museum. The only light in the narrow corridors was an occasional exit sign. It had been six months since the last assault, and if he knew his enemies, this one would be insidious but no less grim. No throat slitting in a public park this time. Amanda's attacker would be smiling. Someone she trusted would rip her throat out.

His high-heeled boots barely echoed as he crossed the Great Hall toward the Arms and Armor galleries. Once inside, Christian stopped to gaze at the daggers, swords, and other medieval weaponry. He was on his way back into the European Sculpture and Decorative Arts galleries when something caught him off guard. As he passed the terracotta statues, marble sculptures, and numerous vitrines full of porcelains and jewels, he thought for a moment he sensed something there; something not mortal. He ran ahead into each smaller gallery, but the feeling dissipated. Occasionally he slipped into the shadows while guards passed him, totally unaware; their voices seemed loud in the quiet spaces. There was no need to avoid the security cameras, since neither his image nor body temperature registered on their screens.

In the main hall, he pushed open a door in the wall and hurried down a dark stairwell toward the curatorial offices. Ruminating over Peter's words 'he is both a night and a day walker' Christian realized that it could only be Ryan's blood that gave the vampire the ability to walk in the daylight, and the only vampire who had had access to Ryan's blood had been Lucien. Michel did not believe Lucien had the audacity or the authority to return to New York, and both vampires guessed that Lucien was dead at the hands of Gaétan and Solange. *Whoever killed him has the blood,* he thought, winding down the familiar hallway and then turning right into Amanda's office.

What a temptation to be able to walk in the daylight.

Christian was always amazed at the stacks of books piled on her floor, her detailed notes, her doodles on a yellow legal pad, and the numerous empty coffee cups. He admired her dedication to art, scholarship, and the written word. Comfortable at her desk he pushed aside several stacks of books, exposing her desk calendar; where various appointments, birthdates, and telephone numbers were neatly written in the squares. He expected no less from her.

He put his feet up on her desk and leaned back to think a moment. He recognized the familiar photograph of her and Ryan with their father. A new one caught his eye. It sat in a dark wooden frame next to her telephone.

Taken on the steps of the Met on a summer day, Amanda sat smiling like a typical ten-year-old girl, shy and awkward. Her long dark hair was parted in the middle and hung almost to her waist. She wore shorts and a tailored blouse. Ryan sat next to her, brooding like a typical bored brother, in jeans and an Eric Clapton T-shirt. *We all need our memories*, he thought, putting the frame down and his feet back up on her desk.

Christian marveled at how little she reminded him of her mother, Catherine Richard, a bohemian woman whose interests in art and politics surpassed her love of her two children. Her sudden death had left Amanda parentless and her fortuitous consolation was her new job at the museum. His heart had broken for her even then; an orphan at such a young age.

He was scanning her office for anything out of the ordinary when her telephone rang. He jumped before he realized that a ringing telephone was a common occurrence despite the hour. She received calls from Europe, and there it was already ten AM. He slid back into her chair, transfixed by her sedate voice projecting around the office, curious about the caller nonetheless.

Hello, you have reached Amanda Perretti at 555–635–1071. I am unavailable at this time. Please leave a message and I will return your call as soon as possible. For immediate assistance please dial Cole Thierry at extension 1070. Thank you.

"Amanda . . . I hope you liked the flowers . . . Thanks again for such an incredible evening . . . sorry I had to leave before you woke up . . . hope you are okay with it all. Talk to you soon. Bye."

Christian's gut twisted as he heard an old familiar voice that made his skin crawl. He slammed his fist on the desk and tried to suppress the jealousy swelling up in him. He had not heard him in centuries, but no, it wasn't possible, and yet, there was no mistaking the raspy, seductive voice.

First Josette and now my Amanda.

He was here in New York. Just as Christian had feared, his enemy had found Amanda, and more than found her. They were lovers. Gaétan had infiltrated her world right under his nose. What kind of a fool was he? *How could I be so unaware?*

He raced out of the museum and made it to his front door just as the pre-dawn sun slipped over the horizon. No matter how hard he fought it, he died every dawn; as if a switch was turned off. Michel, Amanda and even Gaétan would have to wait for sunset as he collapsed onto his bed.

Please God, give me one more day to save her.

Chapter Thirteen

❦

AMANDA WAS CHECKING her e-mails one more time before finishing up for the night.

"Glad I caught you."

Amanda knew the sultry voice before she looked up to find Thomas standing in her doorway, dressed for the night shift. He hesitantly sat down in the only chair in her tiny office.

"Did you get my message?"

She grabbed a catalog and covered her legal pad, not wanting him to see what she was writing or to whom.

"I did, and I loved the flowers." She blushed, feeling a little too vulnerable for her own good as she replayed Saturday night in her mind. She had tried not to spend Monday wondering what to say to him when they ran into one another. She liked him but her heart just wasn't in it. Still, maybe she needed to give the idea of being his lover more time.

"Maybe we could go out this Friday. I have the night off." He picked up a book off her desk.

"Bethany is having a birthday party for her boyfriend, Jeff, at La Crusada over on First Avenue. I would love for you to join me. It's the big three-oh for him." She smiled and twirled a strand of her dark hair.

"I have to be honest with you. I hate dinner parties." He shrugged. "Maybe I could meet up with you afterward."

"Okay. I'm sure we are going bar-hopping afterward." She watched him dust off the cover and open up the old volume, ignoring the white gloves she had pulled out of her desk drawer. No matter how often she reached for the gloves he never put them on. She gave up trying to protect the rare books from further damage.

She watched him, as if in a trance, he ran his hands over the binding, gently turning it over before opening up the book.

"It's definitely rare."

It was rare and brittle and Amanda thought it odd that she had found the book on the floor, especially since she distinctly remembered leaving it atop a stack of other research materials on the other side of her desk. How it had gotten on the floor beside her chair was a mystery.

"Can you translate it?"

'La vie de cour au 18ème siècle France. *Court Life in eighteenth-century France.*" His words rolled over her, confirming her theory that it did not matter what one said in French, anything sounded beautiful.

"Could you take a peek at it for me? Maybe give me the gist of it since your French is impeccable."

"Sure." He shrugged, putting the book down and meeting her gaze.

"Cole asked me to research these objects." She handed him two slides of eighteenth-century porcelains, trying not to be distracted. "Not sure if they are Sevres or something inferior, but they are still so beautiful. Imagine eating dinner off these plates?"

Cole had hired her right out of graduate school as his assistant. Their relationship centered on their mutual love of eighteenth-century France, and need; her need for a prestigious career, and his need to have an assistant that gave him 150 percent. The harder she worked, the better he looked. The better he looked the more work he gave her. They were like parasites, feeding off each other. But she had the utmost respect for him and dreamed of one day being a curator herself. There was almost nothing she wouldn't do for him.

Thomas held each slide up to the light. "Porcelain factories existed in France that made imitation Sevres. Everyone copied the royals and I think that's what you have here."

"Thanks, Thomas." She smiled and touched his hand.

He smiled devilishly and returned the touch. She purposely wore a turtle neck sweater, hoping to cover up the tiny puncture marks on her neck thinking about the night they spent together. *That was some hicky.*

He winked as he slipped out of her office door. At that moment, Amanda wondered why she had invited him to Jeff's birthday party in the first place. He was attractive, smart, great in bed, and they had an easy rapport but she could only think of one person. She could have told him she had plans and left it at that.

Why do I feel so guilty?

She grabbed her legal pad and continued to write the letter she had started earlier.

Dear Christian,

I was hoping you might reconsider your position and speak to me just one more time. I am happy to come to the Grey Wolf.

Amanda

Christian found himself impatiently pacing his living room waiting for Michel to come out of his bedroom for the evening.

"Things are really bad when you are pacing, my friend." Michel joked as he closed the French doors behind him. Christian could not let go of the hilt of his machete, pressed against his chest. As he spoke he kept his eyes on the carpet as he told Michel everything, leaving out the part about Eve accompanying him to Zero Hour. Michel would only chastise him for stooping so low as to get Eve involved in their affairs and he just wasn't in the mood for it.

On more than one occasion, Michel reminded him how ironic he found it that while Christian so vehemently vowed not to interfere in the mortal world he could not help himself when it came to Amanda Perretti. Christian rationalized his covetousness and especially now with Gaétan here in New York he felt justified to snooping around in her personal life. What he called protecting, Michel kindly referred to as stalking.

"I am not stalking her, Michel. I am watching over her. There's a difference," he snapped.

"I just don't see one my friend. It's as if you are in love with her. Are you Christian?"

Christian stopped, shocked at his directness. He half wondered if Michel was joking, but his serious face and quizzical gaze spoke otherwise. Christian tried to avoid looking him in the eye and began to pace again.

Michel gently grabbed his friend by the shoulders. "How do you feel about her?"

"I can't have her . . . it's . . . incestuous. You know that."

"That is not what I am asking you . . . Putting that aside—"

"There is no putting that aside, Michel. I fathered Solange. Amanda is her descendant. How can you even think of such a thing? Christ, we are vampires, not monsters!"

Michel ran a hand through his dark hair, his bright eyes suddenly clouded over, as if all life was drained out of him. In all the centuries of their friendship, he had seen Michel cry only once and even then, he never explained what had upset him so. This was different. Christian felt as though Michel was reliving a memory that was too painful to speak of.

"What is it?" Christian whispered. He could not imagine what would have Michel so shaken. Then the unimaginable crossed his mind. "It's not Amanda, nothing's happened—"

"No, dear God," Michel choked. "She's fine my friend."

Christian stepped back, afraid of his own emotions. Michel straightened his Dior embroidered jacket before he continued.

"I understand the danger Amanda is in from Gaétan. A strike is inevitable, but there is something I must tell you now, before things get... even more complicated ...I know that the heart wants what it wants without reproach or reason—"

Christian grabbed him by his lapels. "Are you trying to tell me you want her?" He hissed, a knot forming in his stomach.

"Christ no," Michel snapped. "All I am saying is . . . it's like the night you met Josette on the Pont Neuf, remember? Your passion for each other was palatable to anyone watching you both."

Christian stared into the dark eyes of his best friend.

"I see it happening with Amanda. Don't deny it, Christian . . ." He stepped back.

"What is it Michel?"

"Josette made me promise." Michel stared past him out the window.

At the mention of her name, memories flooded Christian. Happiness and pain woven together, and then one surfaced. Christian remembered wanting so much to surprise her. Luc Delacore had been away for a fortnight and he had felt the anticipation of having her to himself. He could see himself racing up the stairs into her luxurious apartment near the royal palace in Paris on a bitterly cold March night. It had been snowing hard.

As he entered the salon he had heard her arguing with someone. She was trying to keep her voice low, but with his superior hearing he had clearly heard her fighting, but with whom? As he moved past the ornate Louis XVI furniture and slipped toward her bedroom door, Michel had emerged with Solange on his hip. Christian had been so startled that he had gasped aloud. The crying two-year-old was being comforted by Michel and Christian felt like an intruder watching his friend coddle the child in front of the roaring fire place.

Then Josette had come out of her boudoir behind him. Her beautiful dark hair hung around her shoulders and the dress she wore was everyday, not one of the gorgeous gowns Christian had bought her. She seemed nervous, embarrassed, and guilty. Michel had begun to joke; begging Christian to go out carousing with him, while Josette had taken Solange and excused herself.

Christian had tried to quell the unsettling feeling of something he would not admit, but felt in every ounce of his being. It had been as though he was a spectator, stepping into an intimate moment in the life of a married couple, yet he had thought Josette and Michel were barely acquaintances. When Michel had left to go gambling for the evening, he had stood alone at the fireplace, watching the snow fall, sensing there had been much more between them. Michel had never explained his presence that night and Christian had never asked him for the truth.

"What is it she made you promise, Michel?"

As he asked, he realized that he already knew the truth, just as he had sensed something that night in Josette's apartment. Even that surreal night when both vampires said good-bye to her, he had felt their desire for each other through the smoke and flames. Christian had tried to ignore it, had hoped that time would diminish its power to hurt him.

Michel cleared his throat then blessed himself. "You are not Solange's father, Christian. She had an indiscretion . . . with Gaétan . . ."

Christian stared at him in disbelief.

"Josette knew Solange was his, but she came to me for help since she could not go to him or to you. She feared your wrath. I listened as she weighed it all and in the end she decided to keep the child and say nothing until she was forced to give her up. We both knew you would be the responsible one and you would take care of her."

Michel wiped the corner of his eye.

Christian had to sit down, feeling sick to his stomach.

"I'm sorry. I never wanted to betray her or hurt you. Josette knew you would never forgive her for …seeing Gaétan again, but she also knew you would take good care of Solange, and you did better than that Christian. You have taken care of them all."

"I loved her and trusted her above all others . . ." Christian whispered. "An indiscretion? Oh my God and no one ever told me?"

"Please do not judge her." Michel asked, sitting down beside him.

"I am such a fool Michel . . ."

"No. You are and always have been incredibly loyal to those you love. It made you so happy to follow all these crazy mortals around and it seemed to give you a mission, Christian, and you always needed a purpose in life."

He rubbed Christian's shoulder and he knew Michel was right. He could never tolerate feeling adrift, even as a youth in Meudon, he always worked, always had plans for his day.

"All these years I thought I was preserving something that was mine by rights. How could she sneak around behind my back, especially with him?"

"I don't know what was in her heart, but I do believe their liaison was short-lived. I can't imagine you would be pleased, no matter who she was ... who she was sleeping with."

"And Gaétan . . . if he fathered Solange then he seduced his own daughter?"

Michel shrugged, staring at the ground. "Perhaps he had no idea. But we cannot change any of it, Christian. It's all ancient history as they say."

He smiled and the sparkle in his light eyes returned. He never failed to mesmerize Christian.

"This is true, but Amanda has no idea that our past is coming for her. Am I alone in trying to save her life?"

Michel hugged Christian before the other vampire could react. "You amaze me, my friend. She is nothing to you and yet you continue to honor your promise. You never lost your humanity."

Lost in thought, Christian wondered how Gaétan would strike and if he was he alone. Then another nagging thought made his heart ache. Was the child really Gaétan's or was it Michel's? He had lived his life wondering if they were lovers and yet never able to face that possible truth. It would have changed how he felt about both Josette and Michel and Christian was honest enough to know he would never be able to forgive them. Their indiscretion would have destroyed him then so it was less painful to live a lie.

Chapter Fourteen

⚜

Ross put his phone on speaker as one message after another droned on. Open case files covered his desk underneath his usual dinner of Chicken Quesadillas. The last message was from Christian. It was urgent which made his stomach knot. Something was up and Ross did not understand it which meant it made him angry. It started last summer with Ryan Perretti's gruesome murder and continued with the splay of files on his desk. What linked them to these vampires Ross could not even imagine, but there was a connection.

Although he liked Christian, Ross tried to keep a healthy distance from the other vampires, especially Michel. It was not that he did not get along with Michel. It was more like Michel was a guard dog, forever protecting Christian, although he needed no protecting. Christian refuted Ross's perception that Michel was jealous of their friendship.

Something was happening in a world Ross had only touched on through his friendship with Christian. It was more than supernatural, it was super scary and he preferred to be left out of their business. Vampires monitored their own affairs and remained phantoms in his city which was fine with Ross, but when their prey ended up in a file on his desk, then the lines became blurred and he was forced to investigate.

The body count was growing as the corpses of more homeless people were turning up. Though he had to admit it was alarming, the only thing keeping the city off his back was the fact that the bodies were nameless, faceless indigents. Amanda was right. Nobody gave a crap. Though Ryan was murdered violently, the fact that he was homeless and a heroin addict put him at the bottom of the priority list. His murder would never be solved because there were too many others to take its place.

He had just taken a sip of his coffee and was about to call his girlfriend Melinda, when he felt them enter his office like a wisp of smoke under the door. The overhead switch went off. His desk lamp shed the only light in his office. The growing knot in his stomach just got tighter.

"Detective," Christian purred as he sat down in the wooden chair facing Ross's desk. Michel stood beside him in a floor-length black leather coat. Ross instinctively called the front desk and asked them to hold his calls. He leaned back in his chair and took a sip of his coffee and a deep breath. Melinda would have to wait.

"To what do I owe the honor, gentlemen?"

Christian crossed one leg over his knee. "We need your help."

"You need my help?" He chuckled, taking another sip of coffee. "What is it, another body in a dumpster?"

Neither vampire laughed. He put his coffee cup down and decided to go with his hunch.

"Does this have something to do with all the bodies turning up in the park because I could use some help here myself." He gestured to the files strewn all over his desk.

"Indirectly, yes." Christian flipped his hair behind him. "After we met the other night, I patrolled the entire park looking for anything unusual. I ran across an acquaintance . . . another vampire, who told me an interesting story. Apparently he has made friends with some of the indigents and is panicked now that they are disappearing at such an alarming rate."

Michel interrupted his best friend. "It seems there is a vampire named Thomas who has scared the shit out of some of our kind, which isn't an easy thing to do. Our friend Peter said this vampire just showed up one night."

"Well," Ross shrugged, "if you know who he is, why can't you take care of him?" He took another sip of coffee and put the lid on to keep it warm.

Christian folded his arms across his chest. "It's not that simple, Ross."

Ross studied their masklike faces. He knew full well that nothing was simple in their world. "What am I missing here?"

Michel moved to sit on the edge of his desk, his long legs melting into the shadows. "He's both a night and a day walker."

Ross instinctively reached for a cigarette then stopped himself. "What?" He looked to Christian for validation.

"You remember meeting Peter, Ross? He told me that Thomas has been approaching the homeless men in broad daylight."

Ross had met Peter briefly one night when he was walking with Christian in Central Park. He had had a hard time believing he was a vampire until he picked up a park bench and threw it twenty feet into the air just to demonstrate his prowess. Ross had been duly impressed.

"But I thought it was impossible for vampires to be in the sunlight?"

"We are wondering if Thomas may be a vampire whose real name is Gaétan. Someone, Michel and I knew a long time ago in France. If my hunch is correct then he is responsible for ordering the death of Ryan Perretti and we believe he is now here to slaughter Amanda."

Ross leaned back again. "So why would a vampire from Paris come all to our fair city to murder homeless people, I mean there must be plenty of them in Paris?"

"It's a complicated story, Detective." Michel twirled a strand of his hair.

"I think he works in the Met, Ross—" Christian blurted out.

"The Metropolitan Museum of Art?" Ross shook his head in disbelief. He looked between both vampires.

They stared back at him intently. They weren't joking.

"Not to burst your bubble, but even if I found this guy, I don't have the right to question him without just cause. This is America, remember."

"I know that. I watch CSI and Law & Order." Michel snapped.

"What if I gave you a sketch of him?" Christian asked. "You must have some contacts in the museum? Couldn't you say he was being investigated for....I don't know, something criminal?"

"What about Ms. Perretti?" Ross smiled. "I am sure she would be more than willing to assist you in your investigation."

"She is already involved enough. There has to be a way to get you in there, Ross."

Michel sat down in the other chair in front of Ross's desk, causing Ross to sit back out of fear. "Commit a robbery. Our good friend Detective Ross would have to investigate."

Ross shook his head. "I never heard you say that, Michel."

Christian sat down again, too. "Wait a minute, Ross, Michel has a point. He's there, I can feel it. We just have to flush him out."

"Christian, listen to me—"

"No, you listen to me, Detective. We'll do our part and don't worry. Whatever I take will be returned—"

"I don't want to know, Christian."

Christian reached into his jacket pocket and pulled out a yellow envelope then tossed it across the desk.

Ross opened it carefully after he pulled a pair of reading glasses out of his top shirt pocket.

"He's young and innocent-looking, but he's a monster, Detective." Michel pointed over the detective's shoulder.

"Definitely boyish looking, yeah check out those dimples," Ross joked. The young man in the drawing was model handsome. He had a wide sensual mouth and a devilish smile. His light hair, parted in the middle, fell to his shoulders brushing a lace collar.

"What color are his eyes? How tall is he?" Ross asked grabbing a legal pad.

"His eyes are brown and he's only 5'7"." Michel answered smugly.

"This is professional quality, Christian. Who did this?"

Michel grabbed the sketch from the detective and pointed to Christian. "He was a rich painter with a studio on the Rue de Rivoli."

Christian grabbed the sketch and handed it back to Ross. "Is this enough to go on? He would look exactly the same, only his clothes would be different."

"Yeah, I think I could make a positive ID based on this likeness."

"Good." Christian smiled, towering over Ross. "Don't get too close to him. Just try to get an address on him, find out what he does in the museum, anything we could go on. He has to be living somewhere. Don't try to be heroic. If he can read you, you're dead."

Ross looked up at the towering vampires sheepishly. "How will I know if he can read me?"

"He'll rip your throat out," Michel chuckled. "You won't stand a chance."

Once they were gone, Ross slumped down in his chair, and stared at the drawing, wondering how he had gotten involved in their lives again. Suddenly he gagged and almost missed his waste paper basket.

Chapter Fifteen

❧

AMANDA HAD GIVEN herself twenty-four hours and then decided it was time, yet as she peered out of the idling cab across the street from the Grey Wolf she suddenly had doubts. She had vowed to give it one more chance, and if Christian rejected her . . . well, she would think up something else. The biting wind stung her face as she ran across the street in her high heels.

She felt overdressed, but had feared she would lose her nerve if she stopped at home to change, so she pulled her long wool coat around her to hide her suit. There was no one out front, so she took a deep breath and opened the door. It was early by club standards, only nine o'clock. Loud music blared from the main bar as she scanned the room quickly.

There were a few people at the bar, but no Christian or Michel. The bartender was a tall, moon-faced boy with strawberry blonde hair that just touched his shoulders. As she approached he turned his electric blue eyes on her and she felt herself shake. Maybe this wasn't such a good idea.

"Hi, I'm looking for Christian or Michel."

He scanned her from head to toe, and Amanda wondered if he thought she was from the IRS or some equally terrifying entity.

"And you are?" He asked in a soft voice with a touch of a French accent

"Amanda . . . Amanda Perretti," she replied slowly, annunciating each syllable. A lacy shirt framed his pale chest covered in numerous necklaces. She thought it odd for a man, yet there was nothing feminine about him.

He dropped the towel on the bar and disappeared without a word. She turned away and studied the small group of dancers on the dance floor and the few patrons at the bar. *What's the worst that could happen, he yells at me again?* She glanced down at her watch just as the bartender approached her again.

"He'll be right out. Can I get you a drink?"

"Sure, a glass of Merlot would be great."

She watched him pour, not sure who he was referring to but too full of pride to ask. "So are you a friend of theirs as well?"

"We all go back a long way." He smiled and handed her a drink. "Keep your money, it's on me."

Amanda shoved her money back into her pocket. "Thank you. And you are?"

"Sabin." He nodded, wiping the counter but never taking his eyes off her.

"Bon jour, Ms. Perretti."

She turned to find Michel approaching her. He was wearing a short black jacket and black jeans with each pant leg cut horizontally below the crotch, exposing his long white legs through the shredded black fabric. The look was strangely erotic.

Michel leaned against the bar, studying her. "So, you've come back for more."

"Is he not here or is he avoiding me?"

He smiled down at her. "Both, actually."

"I have to see him again. You're his friend, can't you talk to him?"

Michel laughed, spinning a clean beer glass on the bar.

"If you knew Christian the way I know him, you would understand that once he makes up his mind there is no changing it. What is so important that you can't stay away?"

Amanda took a sip of her wine and a deep breath.

"This may sound crazy but my fate is tied to him."

The beer glass slipped out of his hands and rolled toward her wine glass. Michel tried to grab both glasses before they shattered, but he was too late. Wine spilled and glass flew everywhere as a large chunk sliced his palm.

"Oh my god, you're hurt." Amanda fumbled for a napkin as Sabin tossed him a towel.

Michel wrapped the towel around his hand. "I'll be fine, Amanda, its okay."

Sabin rushed to clean up the broken glass before she could help.

"You might need a couple of stitches. That is one nasty cut."

She tried to take a look, but he pulled his hand away.

"Now where were we my dear?" He sat down next to her, tossing the towel down on the counter.

She impulsively grabbed his hand and turned it over; there was no blood and no gash. "That's strange. It seems to have stopped bleeding."

She looked from Michel to Sabin who said nothing.

"How is that possible?" She tried to get up but Michel grabbed her hand.

"Don't make a scene." He dragged her away from the bar and down a dark hallway. "We must talk privately."

Before she could put up a fight Michel opened a door and gestured for her to enter. "I will answer all your questions. Please step inside... this is our office."

Amanda's heart was racing and she suddenly felt nauseous. *This can't be happening, but it is and I knew there was something different about them. No one's hand can heal like that unless. ...*

Amanda scanned the dark office, keeping an eye on Michel. "I think I need to sit down."

He gestured toward the couch. She took in the modern furniture and the prints of the world's two most famous parks. They were beautiful, but the room was too dark and cave-like for her tastes.

The ticking of the desk clock pulsed in her ears. "How did your hand heal so fast?"

His silence unnerved her as he sat on the edge of the desk. He seemed to hesitate and then he smiled down at her. "I am a vampire, Amanda."

She chuckled nervously as the images of Antoine snarling at her with visible fangs and Lucien tasting her brother's blood came to mind. As unbelievable as it seemed to her, it was the only explanation that made sense.

"Are all of you....I mean Antoine, Lucien....and Christian?" She forced the words out, fearing the truth.

"Don't forget Sabin."

"Oh my God." She stood up, but he beat her to the door.

Her voice caught in her throat. "What do you want from me?"

His strong hands held her steady by her shoulders. "Perhaps the question is what is it you want from Christian?"

She was mesmerized by his green eyes, not sure if trusting him was a good thing, but she had been searching for answers for so long now. "Why did that vampire kill my brother?"

Michel hesitated. "That is not for me to tell you." He brushed a strand of dark hair from her face.

"I need to talk to Christian but since he isn't here I have a letter for him. Will you give it to him..?. Do you really drink blood?"

"We need very little to survive at our age."

She had so many questions; her head was spinning, but she could not formulate the words. To ask questions mean to confirm a reality that both intrigued and terrified her. Amanda had felt as if she had been living a dream since that night in the tunnel. *This really can't be happening to me.* Michel looked no older than she did, but his eyes spoke of pain and experience way beyond the comprehension of a twenty-seven-year-old.

She heard the questions come out before she could suck them back. "How old are you? Where did you come from?"

He paused, staring past her. "Christian and I took our last breath in Meudon, France, on March 3, 1757."

"March third? That's my birthday." Amanda shook as she opened her purse. "Will you take this for me?"

She held a letter in her hands.

"How badly do you want him?"

She felt herself blush as if he had read her mind. "I need to see him Michel."

He ran his fingers through his hair. "Nineteen East 83rd Street. It's a limestone townhouse. Drop it in the brass mail slot. He'll get it. Now go."

Amanda handed the taxi driver the fare and jumped out of the cab on the corner of East 83rd Street and Fifth Avenue. Pulling her coat closer in an attempt to shield herself from the biting wind, she began to walk back up the street. Like a predator stalking its prey, she passed number Nineteen then stopped at the brick townhouse next door. This block was her usual route to the subway, one of the most beautiful streets on the Upper East Side. She passed his house again. *He lives here,* she thought, gathering the nerve to finally stop in front of the gate.

The limestone townhouse was narrow, fitting the architecture of the time, yet elegant with three sets of ascending windows supported by alternating Doric and Corinthian columns. Both the windows and the columns got smaller at the fourth floor, which Amanda presumed was an attic. Its small windows looked like eyes peering down at the passersby.

A room on the first floor was lit up, as was a room on the third floor. For a second she thought she saw Christian peering down at her, framed in the second floor window, but the image was fleeting and she guessed that perhaps it was wishful thinking on her part. Catching her breath, she opened the wrought iron gate and climbed the three steps. She pulled the letter from her purse and went to slip it in the mail slot, then stopped herself.

What harm could it do to ring the bell?

Amanda hesitantly rang the front door bell. Running her tongue over her lips to check if her lipstick was still on, she took another deep breath. She was shivering, although she wasn't sure if it was the cold or her nerves. *Oh my god, suppose he answers the door. What do I say?* She took another deep breath as the front door opened.

"Hi," she smiled, not sure who she was expecting on the other side. He was not much older than she was, with fair skin and faint traces of acne scars on his cheeks. Thin, dirty blond hair that almost matched his skin tone fell to his shoulders. He wore all black with a large silver hoop earring in his left ear.

"Hi, I was wondering if Christian was home. My name is Amanda Perretti. I was just at the Grey Wolf and Michel thought I should drop by to see him in person." She clutched her shoulder bag for support and extended her gloved right hand.

He stood in the doorway, blocking her entry into the warm foyer. "What is it you want?"

"I told you, I want to see Christian if he's home. Please, it's cold out here."

She pushed past him into the dimly lit foyer. The large crystal chandelier looked well over a hundred years old. Light reflected off the crystals onto the shiny, cherry-wood floor, covered with a lush oriental carpet. Marbleized sea green walls surrounded her and the room smelled like an old bookstore, a scent Amanda found familiar.

This is the most beautiful house I have ever been in. It is like a museum.

Lining one wall were some tiny paintings by old masters such as Bernardo Strozzi, Salomon Van Ruysdael, and Jean-Francois De Troy. She stopped in front of a massive still-life painting that hung over a Queen Anne side table. A bust by a French sculptor sat on the table along with various shapes and sizes of ceramic vases.

The waif who let her in came up behind her, leaving the front door open. "You can't come in here. No one is allowed—"

She looked him right in the eye. She had come too far to be turned away by anyone, especially a kid.

"Is he home? If so, get him."

"Who the hell do you think you are to order me around?"

"I'm not leaving until I see him, so scat." She could not believe how brazen she was being, but she was desperate and this kid was not going to scare her away.

She suddenly felt a presence roll up against her, like someone had just turned on a fan. As she turned around there he was standing behind her.

"It's alright, Tony; now close the door, its cold."

Tony sauntered toward the front door and slammed it shut with the back of his hand.

"Hello." He whispered in a soft, deep voice. He was dressed in a pair of brown jeans and a long sleeved white shirt. She noticed that he wore cowboy boots. His clothes appeared so average compared to last night that she had trouble believing what Michel had told her. Maybe he was just a guy with a trust fund that allowed him to collect antiquities and fine art, but she knew better. He was different. The glow from the chandelier illuminated his hair which hid half his face in shadows

"Tony, would you please show Ms. Perretti into the library."

Tony rolled his eyes and led her through a set of French doors into a sitting room with overstuffed furniture, a roaring fireplace, and one entire wall filled with floor-to-ceiling bookshelves. He was gone before she had a chance to chide him for his rude behavior.

Amanda could not get over all the old books. She felt like an addict unable to get enough. First she took one book off the shelf to skim, and then reluctantly put it back, only to grab another to leaf through. There was a book on the French Revolution that she recognized by the title, and another on Marie Antoinette that caught her attention. It did not matter that they were all in French. They called to her from another time and place.

Out of the corner of her eye, Amanda thought she recognized a book she had found on her desk last March. It was written anonymously about the intimate lives of King Louis XVI and Marie Antoinette. She had used it in her research. She impulsively grabbed it off the shelf, wondering if there could be two editions of such a rare book.

She began to flip through it, remembering how difficult it had been to get translated. Her boss Cole had helped her a bit, but had left her with most of it to translate on her own. This was before she had met Thomas, and it had been a difficult project for her. As she turned another page a small yellow piece of paper fell out of the book. It floated down to the carpet like a feather.

Amanda muffled a gasp as she realized that the yellow post-it note had page notations written in pencil in her handwriting. She stuffed the yellow post-it note in her pocket and closed the book, and suddenly, she knew that his presence in her life was not an accident.

Chapter Sixteen

AMANDA WAS ONLY the third mortal ever to come into his home, and he felt strangely vulnerable. He was still trying to wrap his mind around the fact that she was not connected to him by blood and so he no longer had any obligation to protect her. Only his feelings for her kept him bound to her so he would see this through to the end, no matter the outcome.

In his heart, he knew it was about more than a promise he had made to Josette. He wanted Amanda—not her powerful blood, but her love. Now that his conflict over her lineage and his lust was resolvable, he had to protect her and kill his enemy.

Christian stopped just inside the doorway, afraid to come any closer. He folded his arms across his chest and watched her as she put the book away and stepped closer to the fireplace. She was shivering, which he attributed less to the cold and more to nerves. Amanda slowly took off each of her gloves and shoved them in her coat pockets. She rubbed her hands together as she watched him approach.

"Now I understand your reaction to me at the Grey Wolf, but like I told you, I'm not afraid. I just want the truth. I wanted to thank you for saving my life." She continued rubbing her hands together. "Everyone tried to convince me that you didn't exist, but I knew better. I had given up on ever seeing you again, but I always thought of you as my protector, my guardian angel, but Michel tells me differently. He tells me that you are....vampires. Is he joking?"

He was moved by her candidness, her insight, and her seemingly controlled vulnerability. She was like Josette, who despite an arranged marriage and the birth of a child, had managed to maintain lovers and her own independence, all with little fuss. The confines of eighteenth-century life had done little to control her.

"What happened to those other vampires?" She met his gaze as she asked him.

"Antoine turned to dust and Lucien got away."

She nodded, still staring at him. "How is it I was on the grass and not in the tunnel with Ryan?"

"I caught you when you fainted and set you down on the lawn."

He thought she looked poised but ready to bolt at the slightest provocation, so he purposely sat down on the loveseat nearest the fireplace. Christian told himself that if she ran he would not stop her. He thought she was doing a good job of holding herself together. It was not every day that one met a vampire.

"Why did you lie to me at the police station? You don't understand, I thought I was going crazy. No one believed me about ....everything that happened that night."

"Amanda, I apologize but I only did it to protect us both." He flipped his hair behind him. It was so long that it brushed against the sofa seat. "It's not often that mortals come here. In fact, you are only the third person who has been allowed in since 1901. Tony is instructed to act as our guard dog, so forgive his rude behavior. We guard our privacy with a vengeance."

Christian paused, afraid of scaring her away. He weighed every word carefully.

"You were right about Ryan coming into contact with something unusual. He met up with . . . us. He needed money, and there were vampires more than willing to pay him for the one thing they needed: his blood."

"My brother's death was not a random act of violence, was it?" Her question hung in the air between them. Damn Michel for sending her here, and damn him for allowing Amanda into his world. He could not blame Michel; he had tempted her, had led her right to him, and it felt good having her here, as if she belonged with him.

"No, it was not. You need to trust me, as hard as that might be for you. I can't tell you much more about it without exposing you to more danger. Running into you last night was an accident," he lied. "You need to go about your daily life and let me—"

When she touched him he was reminded of how lonely he was, how he missed physical contact and warmth. "Christian, maybe I am missing something here . . . I mean obviously the danger you are trying to protect me from is already here, isn't it?"

Her perception rendered him speechless.

"I'm sorry. I don't mean to be flip. It's just hard to wrap my mind around vampires walking among us, living in New York. I mean . . . all the way here in the cab all I could think about was Michel cutting his hand on a glass and it barely bled, then healed leaving no scar. It all happened in a matter of seconds. Why did this happen to you?"

He picked up a strand of hair and began to twirl it. He liked the way she phrased the age-old question. No one had ever asked him why it happened, yet that was the complicated part, the essence of her question. He liked that about Amanda. She tried to get to the core of a person or a situation. Not that she was judgmental; she just needed to understand him.

"We were two young men who were seduced by the charms of a beautiful woman until it was too late to turn back." He remembered both his and Michel's fascination with Gabrielle. *We were so naïve*, he thought and his mind drifted to one day in particular.

"Did that really happen?" Michel moaned, lying naked across his bed. The early morning sunlight played across his sculpted face and shoulders, making his light green eyes appear to glow.

"All of it and more," Christian said with a smirk. He sat on the end of the bed and tugged at his leather boots. Their eyes locked, and both young men smiled.

"How long have you been awake?" Michel asked as he stumbled toward the tiny room that held the chamber pot.

"It was dark when I awoke," Christian called to his best friend. Michel reemerged and rummaged through his bed linens.

Christian handed him his tattered trousers. "Your shirt is over there." He pointed to the corner as he finished putting on his boots. Michel grabbed his shirt and then poured water from a white porcelain pitcher into a matching bowl; he slowly splashed the water onto his face.

"Now that feels good," he sighed, drying his face on his cotton shirt before slipping it over his head. "Where do you suppose Gabrielle went?"

Michel combed his hair with wet fingers then stretched his neck from side to side.

"I don't know. When I got up she was already gone. I can't remember where she told us she was staying." Christian went to the first-floor French doors and gazed past the courtyard toward the stone well and the stables.

"A very small price to pay for the most incredible night of your young life, don't you think?" Michel chuckled, grabbing his crotch. "I thought it would fall off."

"I'd better go before father realizes I never came home."

"Don't let him intimidate you. You're a grown man, for Christ's sake." Michel tucked his shirt in and looked around for his boots.

"They're under the bed," Christian volunteered, grabbing his coat. "I'll see you later."

"Perhaps we will get lucky again tonight." Michel winked and slapped Christian on the shoulder.

If I never see her again I will consider myself lucky, Christian thought as he stepped out into the courtyard. Something about the bold, dark-haired beauty unnerved him but he could not put his finger on it. The morning air already felt humid and he took a deep breath. He stopped at the well to get water. *How am I supposed to do anything today when I am so exhausted?* He hurried across the courtyard toward the stables to saddle up Starlight, his black mare. As he galloped across the golden fields, he tried to clear his head.

He arrived home and paused in the cuisine, listening for signs of life in his father's house. He had almost made it into the bedroom that he shared with his brother Guillaume when he heard his father's footsteps on the slate floor.

"Are you just coming in, Christian?"

Philippe Du Mauré stood in the dining room with one of their many cats in his arms. He stroked it lovingly. Like his son, he was tall and thin.

"Michel and I went to the Gaspard's last night. I had a bit too much to drink." At best, Christian's relationship with his father was cordial. He always thought he cared more for his cats than he did for his sons.

"I hope she was worth it," he snapped, turning on his heels and walking away. Christian began to say something, but stopped himself. He was grateful that his father had spared him another lecture concerning his whoring with Michel. He dreaded working in the hot sun, feeling hung over with so little sleep, but he threw his coat down on his bed and went over to his washbasin to clean up nevertheless. *Yes, I hope she was worth it, too,* he thought, noticing the two small wounds on his neck in the faded mirror. *What has she done to me?*

"Were you in love with her?" She stared up at him with eyes that took his breath away.

"As much as any of us could know about love at twenty years old."

"Twenty! Who was she?"

"Her name was Gabrielle."

"God, I'm almost thirty and I still haven't figured love out yet." She smiled up at him.

"Don't tell me there's no one special in your life?"

"There is . . . sort of . . .There's this ongoing joke in our department about the mysterious books that show up just around the time my boss Cole dumps a major research project on me. Though the books are helpful, my French is horrible and I turn to either Cole or . . . this friend to help with the translations."

"It sounds like Cole is quite the taskmaster."

"He is . . . the man is brilliant, but very busy, so I turn to a friend for help. He's a night guard at the museum, actually, but he's also French, and he knows more about the French Revolution than any textbook I have ever read. He's . . . incredible."

Christian reached up and touched her face with his fingertips. Her skin was warm and she seemed so willing. Her scent was intoxicating. He closed his eyes and took in a deep breath, as if he were surrendering to a dark current, never to surface again.

"You want incredible?" He whispered, pulling her into his arms.

She froze as he gently kissed her warm lips. He lifted her chin towards him to breathe in her scent. He could not trust himself to let her go. It was wrong, he had to protect her.

"You'd better go now." His breath caught in his throat as he pulled away from her.

"Why?" She asked holding onto him. He could read the lust and confusion in her face. He left the room before she could ask any more questions, and he stopped on the second floor when the front door slammed. It echoed through the silent house and his soul. He watched from the window as she walked to the corner of Fifth Avenue to hail a cab. It had taken all his will to make her leave, but there was something he had to find out before he was too late.

Chapter Seventeen

IT WAS WELL after midnight, early Wednesday morning when Christian entered the Metropolitan Museum of Art. His footsteps made no sound as he cut through the labyrinth of galleries in the Egyptian Wing then through the Temple of Dendur in the Sackler Wing. The vampire planned to start on the first floor and work his way upstairs to the American Wing.

If he's here, I will find him.

He knew the guards had a set routine that rarely varied. They worked in pairs and made their rounds on the hour. As he walked, he began to second guess himself. Was that Gaétan who had left a message on Amanda's answering machine? It had sounded like the ancient vampire, but it had been centuries since he heard him speak. He needed more proof and this was the place to find it.

The thought of him making love to Amanda was too much to bear. He felt rage build up inside of him as he cut back through the Arms and Armor galleries where he heard voices and laughter. As he entered the Equestrian Court, two guards sat on the dais under a knight on horseback, their sandwiches and coffee spread out between them. They were talking sports, and he moved past them undetected.

Christian scoured the entire museum and found nothing unusual. Guards in pairs made their rounds just as they always did, but there was no sign of anything or anyone out of the ordinary.

Maybe I am losing my mind after all, he thought as he sat down on the bed in the Louis XVI bedroom in the French furniture galleries. It was time to think and formulate a plan and this room felt so much like home with its delicate chairs, Marie Antoinette desk and pale green walls.

He closed his eyes and put his face in his hands, trying to concentrate in the deathly quiet of the museum. He had never taken the older vampire seriously while stealing his mortal lover, Josette Delacore right out from under his nose. Michel had always tried to protect him, especially when it came to Gaétan. They never knew where he had come from, only that he was at least two hundred years old when he emerged on the social scene in Paris. Christian's memory tumbled over a night hundreds of years ago when Michel had tried to warn him about the powerful vampire, but he was too arrogant, too full of hope.

He had crept into the parlor of the apartment they both shared with Gabrielle, silently closing the French doors behind him. As he turned he realized he was not alone. Michel sat on a divan in the far corner of the room, half hidden in the shadows cast by the torchieres. He seemed uncomfortable, stretched across a delicate couch, wearing nothing but satin britches.

"And where have you been all evening?" Christian could hear the anger underneath Michel's words.

There was no use in lying. Michel had already smelled the mortal woman on him.

"Where's Gabrielle?" Christian asked, though he could have guessed.

"Where we all were and you should have been tonight, at the salon of Madame Troustes." He held Christian's gaze.

"I had other business to attend to this evening."

Michel was in front of him before he could take another breath. "She belongs to Gaétan. Do you have a death wish?"

Christian shrugged. "He will grow bored of her soon enough—"

Suddenly Michel was circling him. "So, use your head. Let him tire of her and discard her. Then there is no further animosity between you."

He knew Michel was only trying to protect him, and he was right, but it was no use. He had become bewitched by Josette Delacore. Ever since the night they had met on the Pont Neuf he wanted her. Tonight they had walked alone near her apartment on the Seine.

"I cannot wait that long Michel. I can't stay away from her. She is —"

"She is a child, Christian. She knows not what she plays with and I am only trying to save your life."

Christian tried to move past him. "It's too late for that Michel."

"Listen to me." Michel grabbed his friend by his frock coat. "He will not harm her, but come after you." He poked Christian in the chest. "I like my eternal life, how about you?"

"She said she would leave him for me."

Michel's mouth fell open.

"That's right and I refuse to wait for that cunning bastard to try to talk her out of it."

Michel shook his head. "You play with fate, my friend."

"If she walks away from him he will act as though it does not matter—"

"True, but it does and he will wait for the right moment to strike back at you." Michel put an arm around his friend.

"I know you mean well." Christian tried to smile as he thought about the lie he would have to concoct for Gabrielle.

"He will get his revenge Christian, you'll see."

The two sets of male voices brought him back to the present. They were coming towards him from a gallery down the hall. Christian quickly retreated back down a corridor and waited in the shadows as they approached. He quietly slid his machete out of the sheath and waited for them to come into view. He held his breath as two figures emerged from the shadows approaching him. Their voices booming in the silence as their footsteps echoed in the cavernous hallway.

In a moment he realized the guard on the left was Gaétan. He barely felt him, nor did he recognize the vampire. It was as if he no longer was immortal.

It must be the blood that shields him.

He seemed shorter than Christian remembered, but then he realized that people in this century were taller by comparison. His long hair was now shoulder-length and tied back in a ponytail. He wore the typical blue uniform of a museum guard, complete with an ID badge, a walkie talkie, a set of keys, and a flashlight. He laughed at something the other guard, a taller Hispanic man said, and Christian wondered if his enemy could sense his presence. For a second he wanted to rush him, thinking he could take his head if he acted fast enough, but then he stopped himself.

He glanced up at the cameras all around the galleries and realized that Gaétan was able to appear on camera without drawing suspicion. He seemed so ordinary, in fact, that Christian had a moment of doubt. He wondered if he had made a mistake and it was his imagination that was in overdrive. He watched them walk slowly down a corridor, still talking and then they made a sharp right.

Christian followed them until they reached a bank of elevators. Gaétan got on his walkie talkie and let someone know they were taking a break. The elevator doors opened and they both stepped inside, then Gaétan quickly stepped outside again, calling to the other guard to hold the elevator door.

Christian moved further into the shadows as Gaétan shone his flashlight into the recesses around the elevator. It was hard for Christian to believe it was really him but when he spoke, his voice removed any doubt.

Christian raised his machete in case the vampire came toward him and waited for what seemed like hours.

Once satisfied, the other vampire got back inside the elevator and the doors shut.

Christian fell to his knees, trying to stay calm. He could not believe his own eyes but it was true. His ancient enemy was here, working in the museum with Amanda. She was more of a threat to the Parisian vampires than he had ever imagined and there was no more time. He had to get moving and execute his plan.

Racing down the grand staircase and back through the medieval galleries he stopped at the French period rooms again. From there he slowly walked towards the case of beautiful terra cotta statutes from eighteenth century France. They were small, perhaps fifteen inches high. One would be easy to carry away.

Needing to suppress his strength he gently hit the glass case. It bowed inward then unable to take the pressure, it shattered in a web- like pattern. Shards of glass tore the leather sleeve of his duster. Quickly he grabbed a statue and tucked it into his coat while the alarm pierced the silence. Not sure how much time he had before the guards would converge in the gallery, he ran towards the Great Hall and the exit.

Christian found himself on the south shore of the reservoir. Black water glistened under the street lamps, casting his ominous reflection back to him. Passing the Central Park precinct, he thought about stopping in to see Ross, but he didn't need to talk, he needed to squelch the rage inside him. He wound north around the reservoir until he was calm enough to think clearly again. His long strides made no sound as he headed toward the loch in the North Woods. He passed no one.

As he came through the Glen Span Arch, the stench of someone up ahead stopped him. He scanned the bare landscape but saw nothing. Then he noticed a young man sitting on a rock on the banks of the Loch, almost hidden by the boulders. The roar of the icy water made his approach undetectable as he came toward the boy. The boy sat cross-legged, his face half hidden by his hooded sweatshirt. His black jeans were torn and he smelled dirty, but his blood smelled sweet to the vampire.

Christian waited, poised in a copse of trees as the urchin tried to stand up. He wobbled and fell face first into the rushing water. He reminded Christian of a bear trying to catch a salmon. Christian watched as he tried again to get up and fell into the water. Slowly, he stood up, teetering a bit yet managing to stay upright. Christian watched, initially amused at the young mortal, then he felt his amusement turn to frustration and anger.

Why had he sent Amanda away? Why was he so afraid to be with a woman again? It had always been so easy for Michel to take lovers, and even in his youth, Christian had many women. The need for both blood and sex drove him to hunt them down and take their bodies and their blood. He had not loved them; he preyed on them. Josette had been the love of his life and he had left her to die, mortal and alone. Why?

Selfishly, Christian did not like vampires, especially the female of the species. He wanted a mortal woman by his side. It was crazy he knew, but there was something wrong, something that kept him alone and so lonely.

In a blind rage, the vampire grabbed the boy by the collar and yanked him off the ground. He slammed him back onto the rocks and heard something crack as the boy moaned and rolled into the water. Christian yanked his limp wet body up out of the water, his right arm dangling like a rag doll. He pulled the boy into his dark eyes and willed him to be still. Then he bit into the cold mortal's neck; the warm blood gushed into his mouth and ran down his throat. The boy tried to fight him, but it was useless. His screams were muffled by the icy water roaring beside them.

Taking human life, especially in anger, seemed irrational and irresponsible to Christian, but tonight he did not care; he felt powerless. How could he not tell Amanda the truth about Gaétan? Maybe he had taken the wrong approach all along. Maybe she could help him find his enemy and together they could bring him down.

He sucked harder as the boy's heart pounded, fighting for survival. Then it began to slow down. Christian stopped himself as the boy died in his arms and then let him go, dropping him like a leaf into the rushing water. Something about his lifeless eyes chilled even the vampire.

Christian opened the door of his townhouse. Her smell lingered, a reminder that she had really been there. He needed time to think. Everything was happening so fast.

He put the machete down beside him on the couch and leaned back. Sated with so much mortal blood, he felt comforted and safe. The fire warmed him and he closed his eyes; his thoughts turned from the women in his present to the woman from his past, Josette Delacore.

"Aren't you going to introduce me, Gaétan?"

Gaétan feigned a smile, but Christian knew he was fuming inside. She extended her hand and he took it cautiously, kissing her gently. He could feel her shudder as their eyes locked.

"Josette Delacore, this is Christian Du Mauré, who is usually by the side of Gabrielle. By the way, where is she tonight?"

Michel rolled his eyes at his best friend.

"We are meeting up at Madame Troustes later to hear some opera music," he confessed, unable to take his eyes off the young beauty before him. She was petite, with smooth white skin that glistened in the torch light that lined the bridge. Her silk dress shimmered and she smelled intoxicating. Christian thought her eyes were the darkest green he had ever seen. They were warm and seductive, intelligent and kind. Her smile was wide, and her high cheekbones were framed with dark curls.

At that moment all he wanted was to know her, to taste her and hear her cry out his name in pleasure. Nothing else mattered except possessing her. It was not vampiric seduction on his part, but instant love for the young vampire.

"My, a cultured vampire; how refreshing." She smiled, but did not pull her hand away.

"Would you like to hear opera music tonight, my love?" Gaétan begged, taking her hand from Christian's.

She looked from one vampire to another. "Why don't we all go?"

Christian smiled to himself as he tossed another log on the fire. That had been a part of Josette's charm. She was fearless, with no guile or shame. Had she betrayed him and taken Gaétan back as her lover, or had someone so close to him that he was like a brother fallen in love with her as well? He could not blame Michel if he had fallen in love with her, nor could he confront Josette. She had accepted them on their terms without sacrificing her own life. Like Amanda, who only wanted to understand them, Josette had never been afraid of the vampires she had taken as her lovers.

The front door clicked just before dawn. The French doors opened and closed silently as his best friend crept into the room. No human would have heard his approach. Christian had been sprawled out on the couch for hours, gazing into the fire and trying to imagine what was happening at the museum at that moment. Amanda's kiss kept distracting him. Michel sat down in an overstuffed chair near the couch.

"I see you let her in this time." Michel had smelled her as soon as he opened the front door. "How long before you chased her out?"

Christian rolled his eyes at his best friend, but he knew him better than anyone.

"What the hell are you wearing, Michel? Christ, you look like a satanic ostrich."

Michel jumped up and twirled around to show off his short jacket and his black jeans with the pants legs cut horizontally.

He smiled devilishly. "It fits my persona, don't you think?"

Christian begged him to sit down and gave him the details of his visit with Amanda. Michel listened intently, not surprised at her intuitiveness, and only rolled his eyes once when Christian described kissing her then making her leave him. Christian purposely waited until almost dawn to tell Michel that he found Gaétan at work in the museum and that he had executed their plan. He directed Michel to the mantle, where a terra cotta figurine sat crammed between his authentic collection of Ming vases.

Michel picked it up and closely studied the valuable sculpture as Christian reminded him that all they had to do was to wait, be patient, and let the mortals and their laws do the rest. He reminded Michel that he was keeping Amanda out of danger this way. As he retired for the night, he wondered if he wasn't trying to convince himself. Perhaps he had too much faith in Ross and the mortal world. Gaétan's presence scared Christian, although he would never admit that to Michel. Whether Gaétan meant to take Amanda back to Paris or he had fallen for her remained unclear to him.

He found it ironic that they had shared three of the same women. It was too bad there had been such hate between them. He wondered how Amanda felt about her friend, Thomas. Did she love him, or was he just a good lover? The difference was not lost on him as he turned on his side and stared at the machete he kept by his bedside.

As the sun rose, he could not help but dwell on Gaétan being able to walk around in the daylight while he could do nothing. He tried to imagine what the sun would feel like on his face, what it would be like to see the blue sky again, but the memories eluded him. If he took some of her blood, he could experience it, too, but at what price? He would have to wait until nightfall to take part in the drama at the museum. His last thought as he drifted off was of Amanda, her beautiful eyes closed, anticipating his kiss. He tried not to feel too hopeful.

Once at home, Amanda took a long hot shower and then she crawled into bed. Lying in the darkness, Amanda thought about her conversation with Christian and how his kiss had made her feel. She wondered about the vampiress Gabrielle, and how incredible it must have been for her to have both Christian and Michel as her lovers. The fantasy aroused her but she was too tired to think much more about it.

She noticed the tiny green light flashing from her desk and jumped up. She had forgotten to check her cell phone voice mail. There were two messages. One was from Bethany, telling her there had been a change of venue for Jeff's birthday celebration. At the insistence of one of Jeff's friends, the after-dinner festivities were taking place at this weird club he had heard about, the Grey Wolf. Bethany did not sound thrilled, but commented that Amanda might be, especially if that rude guy was there. She meant Christian of course.

The second message was from Thomas and he definitely wanted to be counted in for the after-dinner party on Friday night.

Suppose Christian is at the Grey Wolf as well?

Amanda wondered whether she would be happy with Thomas if Christian had not come into her life. Perhaps, but meeting Christian had changed everything. She had found the man of her dreams and he was all that she wanted. There was no turning away from him no matter what he was.

Chapter Eighteen

Ross CHECKED HIS watch again; it was only two in the morning but it felt like noon. He was so looking forward to having the next two days off he could not wait for his shift to end. Four more hours and he would be on his way home. He had promised Melinda they would go over to New Jersey and down to Atlantic City to do some serious gambling. Though it was premature, the detective began to put away the numerous files that littered his desk. The homeless would have to wait until next week.

He had just come back into his office from the records room when the alarm went off. His heard Briggs yelling as he ran down the hallway towards Ross, "Jesus Christ, it's the Met."

Ross grabbed his jacket and his gun, and ran down the hall. As the officers took off on foot toward Fifth Avenue, Ross shivered.

Son of a bitch, he really did it.

Gaétan and Lazarra had just sat down with their coffee when the code came over their walkie talkies. Gaétan froze, and Lazarra almost spilled his coffee all over the table, cursing at no one. Both guards had read and rehearsed for such an event, but at that moment they were paralyzed, unsure of what to do. Gaétan watched as Lazarra wiped up his coffee and tried not to panic himself. He knew museum protocol; there would be a lockdown and no one would be allowed to leave until security had cleared them.

Gaétan had almost none of Ryan's blood left. Though he was older and needed little to survive, he still craved hunting and killing mortals. Taking their blood was almost secondary to killing them for sport. The kill had even more appeal for him. He checked his watch: 3:05 AM. Hopefully he could stay calm for the next few hours while he was questioned.

He thought he felt something close by just before he and Lazarra had gotten into the elevator; one of his own kind, perhaps? He had found recently that he was losing his ability to sense or smell the presence of another vampire. Had Solange finally followed him to New York to seek her revenge on him like a scorned lover, or had Christian discovered his real identity? Scarier to him than this reality was his reaction to it. He kept telling himself he would slaughter Amanda when the time came and replenish his diminishing supply of blood.

He was meeting her on Friday night. Perhaps then he would make his move and take her back to Paris as he had originally planned, yet the world of the Parisian vampires seemed so far away and no longer a part of his life. It was all so confusing and Gaétan was no longer sure of his destiny. He quickly followed Lazarra upstairs to the Great Hall for further instructions.

❦

"Hello," Amanda murmured into her cell phone. It was 5:30 AM.

"Amanda, its Cole, sorry to have to wake you up like this but there's been a break in at the Met."

It took her a moment to realize it was her boss calling her. "What?"

She rolled over and tried to clear her head.

"There's been a robbery Amanda. I'm on my way over there right now."

"When? Oh my God." She reached over to turn on the light on her end table. It was hard to think in the darkness.

"All I know is that our galleries have been robbed," he replied, his voice holding just a hint of disbelief.

"What was taken?" Amanda stared down at the floral pattern in her pajamas, trying to make sense of it.

"I don't have any details." Cole sounded stunned. "All I know is that the alarm went off and two museum guards responded. The call went right to the Central Park precinct. I am on my way over there now."

Amanda's thoughts were racing as she lay back down. Who would dare try to steal anything from one of the most prestigious and revered, not to mention well-protected, art institutions in the world? The Met had one of the most advanced security systems on the market. She impulsively flipped on the news, wondering if the story had gone public, but found nothing.

When she realized she was not going to fall asleep again, Amanda decided to check her e-mails. She had just turned on her computer when the phone rang again.

"Hi, it's me. You need to come over right away."

"How bad is it, Cole?"

"All I have been told is that it was as neat as a pin."

"I'll be right there."

Amanda tried to get a read on the situation from Cole's voice.

"The police need to question our department. They'll let you in at the 84th Street entrance and then direct you where to go, okay?"

As she turned on the hot water, she thought about Thomas. He was working the night shift. He had to know about it. She debated calling him, but then stopped herself. She imagined he would be questioned, too, along with all the guards on shift. After taking a record-breaking five-minute shower, Amanda threw on a pair of brown woolen pants and a white cotton sweater. She quickly dried her hair and applied lipstick and eye shadow. She thought that the face in the mirror looked older and more guarded than the woman she remembered staring back at her last summer.

After squirting on her favorite perfume and putting on a pair of silver earrings, she grabbed her purse and her coat. The number Six train heading uptown was already crowded, but she managed to find a seat. The sun was already up when she came out of the subway onto Lexington and 86th. She called Bethany as she walked towards the museum, and left a detailed message about the events there. She also expressed her disbelief that the party plans had been changed, but said that she would speak to Thomas.

He is only three blocks away, she thought, heading down Fifth Avenue. *Does he sleep in a coffin? I can't believe he lives right here. He has always been so close.* She flashed her ID and passed through the security booth before stopping to glance at her watch: 6:30 AM. It already felt like a long day.

She was directed to the first bank of elevators. The operator nodded hello and then pressed the button for the fourth floor: conference room 4B. She nodded back. It was too early to make small talk. Although being questioned was standard procedure in an investigation like this one, she still had a large knot in her stomach.

I guess I'll find out now, she thought, knocking gingerly on the light wooden door with the gold letters *4B* emblazoned on the front. It opened quickly. Bob Hart, the museum's head of security, stood in the doorway.

He looks tired, she thought as she entered the room, blinded by the white lights.

They were baffled. No matter how many times the security department replayed the tapes the same image appeared on the screen; a flicker of brilliant light and then the smashed case. Numerous small screens covered the walls of the small, dark security office, but Bob Hart, Detective Burt Ross, Sergeant William Briggs, and Jean Paul Rènard, Director of the Metropolitan Museum of Art, stood staring at one screen in particular.

At 03:00 hours nothing was amiss and the case was intact. Then a blinding flash of light and a muffled sound like a hand hitting cardboard. The time: 03:01 hours. Bob Hart had already begun to question all guards on the night shift. Once the alarm had gone off and the police had arrived no one had was allowed to leave until they had been cleared by the NYPD.

"It's like a phantom was there." Sergeant Briggs kept commenting, scratching his head.

Or a vampire, Ross thought, as he watched the tape over and over.

Amanda had returned to her desk around eleven AM, just in time to check her voice mail messages before being summoned to Cole's office down the hall. She sat down in a faux Louis XVI chair, the only other piece of furniture in his tiny office beside a large wooden desk and shelves of books.

The questioning had been grueling and Amanda felt mentally exhausted. No matter how many times she went over her daily schedule, after a while she even began to second guess herself. She knew she had nothing to hide. She tried to imagine what had been stolen. It felt like a dream. Staring up at one of Cole's photographs of the Latin Quarter in Paris she imagined walking there with Christian on a beautiful summer night.

"Amanda, are you alright?" Cole's voice broke her reverie and brought her back to the present.

"I'm just a little tired, that's all. Being questioned like that is exhausting. Even if you know you're innocent, you begin to doubt yourself."

"Bob just called me. There are no prints, nothing on camera, just a vitrine with an eight-inch hole in it," Cole explained, shaking his head unable to share with her what had been stolen.

"The police will find something." She noticed how tired he looked. "What about the Louvre, are they still sending the desk?"

Their department was mounting an exhibition to open in a few weeks which included a rare writing desk owned by Marie Antoinette.

"Jean Paul has been on the phone with them himself all morning. I suppose they could rescind."

Cole was the most serious man she had ever known. At first she had thought it was their age difference, but as she got to know him better, she realized that Cole Thierry was just born old. She considered it a personal triumph if she got him to laugh. Though she did not consider herself the most lighthearted person, she felt like a standup comedian compared to him.

"I can't believe it's time to think about that dinner dance again." Amanda tried to distract him.

"I know." He rolled his eyes and picked up a stack of papers. "I'd better try to get some work done here."

Just then Bob Hart appeared in the doorway.

"Sorry to interrupt, Cole. Could I speak to you for a minute?"

Amanda headed back to her office to try and get some work done. It was hard to stay focused, so she gave up after an hour. She restacked the books in the "to read" pile on her floor, and then sat back to relax just as her cell phone rang. It was Bethany.

"Holy shit, Amanda. What's going on over there?"

"I really can't say much about it, but there was a robbery."

They spoke briefly and Amanda promised to call her later and was again interrupted by her office phone.

"Amanda Perretti." She answered curtly.

"Did they put you under the hot lights and sweat a confession out of you?" Thomas asked in his heaviest French accent.

"Oh yeah, but I think I passed with flying colors. How about you?"

"I think I passed. How is the infamous curator handling all this?"

"Oh, you know Cole, grace under pressure as always. He tries not to show it, but he's really upset. He can't help but take it personally."

"Is the Louvre still sending the desk?"

"I don't know."

"Hey, are we still on for Friday night?"

"There's been a slight change in plans. One of Jeff's friends convinced him to go to this club in the West Village called the Grey Wolf, or something like that." She feigned playing dumb to cover up her guilt. She was the world's worse liar, but she could manage it better over the phone.

When she heard nothing, she thought he might have hung up or perhaps they had been disconnected.

"Thomas, are you still there?"

Amanda held on to her cell phone and listened to the silence.

Chapter Nineteen

ROSS WAS DYING for a fresh cup of coffee. He had been cocooned in the museum all day, interviewing any staff connected to the department, including security and maintenance personnel. It was now six in the evening. He was back in his office at the precinct trying to sort through his notes and regroup from the day. In the men's room he splashed some cold water on his face, shaken over the deception he felt a part of.

He had left a message for Christian explaining that he had interviewed a Thomas Bretagne and he wondered if this was the vampire they were looking for then placed a call to Melinda to let her know their weekend in Atlantic City was probably off. Ross thought about getting some dinner when Briggs stopped in. A boy's body had been found on the shores of the loch and he was on his way to check it out.

Homicide had identified one David Hensen from Montclair, New Jersey. The boy had been drained of all blood, which matched the same MO as all the other homeless victims, only this kid was a college student. Ross went to the precinct door and wondered if more snow was in the forecast. He hated winter and anything to do with it and vowed every year to move to Florida. He imagined himself walking a beat in South Beach or Ft. Lauderdale.

By the time he finished all his paperwork and checked in with Briggs it was midnight, Thursday morning. He had read the preliminary report on Mr. Hensen, studied the photographs and decided to call it a night. There was nothing more to be done. Ross said goodnight to Briggs and headed home, east on the 85th street transverse. He loved to walk and tonight, despite the cold he needed to clear his head and suck down a few cigarettes on his way home. An occasional jogger passed, bundled up against the winter chill, but otherwise he was alone. He lit a cigarette and began to sort through the clues from the murder at the loch. It had to be the same perpetrator, who was offing the homeless.

Yeah, the total blood loss would point to a vampire, Ross. Call a spade a spade.

He was still spooked over this Thomas Bretagne. Was he the vampire Christian was hunting for? He instinctively moved to his right to let a jogger pass then flicked his cigarette butt.

Ross regretted getting involved in the vampire world, but he had crimes to solve, yet Christian had asked for his help which made him feel just a bit frightened. He felt another jogger come up behind him and moved to the right only no one passed him. Instinctively, Ross reached for his gun as he turned around but someone grabbed him with such force he was knocked to the ground.

He fought back but the mugger had him pinned to the ground so fast he had no time to defend himself. The last thing Ross remembered was falling into a pair of familiar dark eyes.

Ross slowly woke up. His head was pounding and he was lying on something hard and cold. He felt nauseous and his right arm seemed numb. He could hear the faint sound of cars in the distance.

"Make a move and I crush your hand, Detective." He could see the faint outline of someone standing over him. His long coat flapped in the cold breeze.

Ross's right hand was throbbing. As his eyes adjusted he realized that the stranger had one foot on his hand and then he knew who it was and why he was here. He had been found out.

"What do you want, Thomas?" Ross stuttered through a dry throat.

"Now, Detective, let's not be coy. You know who I am and why you are here."

Though Thomas was slight, Ross knew he could crush his hand and more if provoked further. It was no use trying to reach for his gun, it was gone, and his hand was wedged under the vampire's stylish boot. His odds were looking grimmer.

The wind had picked up and Ross noticed a flag waving in the sky behind the vampire. Could they be atop Blockhouse No. 1 in the northern end of Central Park? Thomas must have carried him there.

The vampire squatted down over Ross. He smiled and exposed his fangs. Ross broke into a sweat. He was trapped and utterly defenseless.

"He's your friend, isn't he?"

Ross felt the seductive power of the vampire's words move over him in waves. He tried not to scream when Thomas pulled him to an upright sitting position by his hair. Then he saw the knife.

"This can be easy or this can be hard, Detective. Now tell me why he has you sniffing around me like a puppy dog." Gaétan waved the knife past his face.

"I don't know who you are talking about—"

"Come on, Detective. I know you two are friends and that you're connected to the mortal girl as well. I can read your thoughts, remember?"

"If you can read my thoughts then why the stupid questions?"

The pain was excruciating as every bone in his hand exploded. Ross heard himself scream as the vampire ground his hand into the stone. Blood and bone leaked out from under his boot.

"Oh, God," Ross moaned. The pain made him so nauseous he almost passed out.

"Tell me brave Detective Ross, were you a part of Christian's plan or are you just his lackey?"

"Don't patronize me you bastard . . ." Ross fought back trying to pull his hand out from under Thomas's boot.

"If you ever want to see your precious Melinda or Florida ever again, talk to me." The vampire growled in his face.

Ross suddenly was back on the playground at his old grammar school. Constantly picked on for his ethnicity and dark good looks he had made a reputation for himself as a bully, but he did not see it this way at all. He was protecting his honor from brats with no guts or self-esteem. The only way they could take him down was to jump him, to catch him unaware.

This vampire was no better than a bully who had jumped him from behind, not giving Ross a fair fight. He would not let Ross go, no matter what he confessed. There was only one thing left to do.

"So Detective, what is your role in all this?"

He stared down at Ross with a smile that made the detective sick. He would never use his right hand again and in all likelihood, he would never see the light of day again. It was immature, but it was all he had left.

Thomas growled as the spittle ran down his face and then the vampire was on him. Pain exploded in Ross's gut as the knife tore through him. He felt his body go limp but Thomas held him up by his hair. The knife pierced his stomach again then slid up through his rib cage. Ross felt himself growing colder as his warm blood ran down his legs. The vampire tossed the knife and as Ross drifted into unconsciousness, the vampire buried his face in his warm blood and drank.

Chapter Twenty

⚜

Good evening my old friends,

It is Étienne calling from Paris. It is February first. You are probably wondering how I found you both and why I am calling you after all this time. Gaétan called a meeting in his apartment last summer. I accompanied Gabrielle and met with both he and.....Solange. He told us about Lucien coming to New York City and his experience with the mortal boy at your club. He also told us about the girl, Amanda. Gaétan led us to believe that her blood was a threat to our kind. Gabrielle sanctioned his plan to come to New York himself to kill the girl. He should have been home by now but there has been no sign of him. We have heard rumors that Solange has threatened to come herself to finish the job she fears Gaétan has failed to do. Lucien disappeared shortly after coming home. Gabrielle and I believe Gaétan murdered him and has whatever blood Lucien had brought back with him. You know I have never trusted them. Not since the old days has there been so much mistrust among us and the threat of war is in the air again. No one knows that I have contacted you. I fear even Gabrielle would take it as a sign of weakness, or worse, you know how she is. I miss you both so much and I think about the old days on the Rue de Rivoli when the four of us were together. Your friend forever. Étienne.

Christian played the message for the third time. It had been centuries since he had heard the soft spoken voice of their old friend, Étienne. He sat down in the leather chair and twirled from side to side still in disbelief about the presence that filled the office. Michel had come in to take care of some paperwork and noticed the flashing red light. He had hit the button just as Christian had come in, and Étienne's voice had filled their ears.

After the third listen, Christian got up and went to stand before the antique map of the Bois du Boulogne. His thoughts raced back to a hot summer night in 1780.

Christian and Michel had just finished feeding on drunken prostitutes, a pleasure Michel never tired of, and were wandering in the park. The air was crisp and clear for a summer night, and the chirping of crickets was deafening. Christian looked up at the full moon, marveling in its beauty. The night sky was clear and full of stars. The two vampires strolled along together in silence, their leather boots making no sound in the dirt.

"I think we have company," Michel whispered, feeling the faint reverberation of footsteps behind them. "Someone is following us."

"Who would follow *us*?" Christian asked arrogantly, hearing only the sound of the crickets.

Michel turned abruptly and spotted someone standing in the shadows.

"A smelly boy," he murmured under his breath, getting wind of his body stench. "Well, what have we here?" Michel asked Christian, stopping a few feet away from the boy, who blended into the shadows cast by the trees.

"Can we help you with something?" Christian politely asked the trembling boy.

"I am starving," the boy explained, studying first Christian and then Michel.

"You have no home?" Michel asked, crinkling his nose up at the boy.

"We could not pay the rent and lost our business. We bartered everything we had. Now we are homeless." He never took his eyes off both of them.

"Ah, another bunch of *sans-culottes*," Michel sneered arrogantly.

Christian knew the child was afraid and desperate, yet his voice never quivered as he spoke to them. *He is so thin, he probably hasn't eaten in days*, Christian thought. *His clothes are filthy, yet he holds himself like an aristocrat; he has a regal manner about him.*

"Michel, we are forgetting our manners," Christian replied, studying the boy carefully. He was of average height, with wavy hair that looked to be brown.

"I am Christian Du Mauré, and this is Michel Baptiste." He nodded toward the other vampire. Michel rolled his eyes at Christian.

"My name is Étienne Forneau." The boy nodded, glancing first at Christian and then Michel.

"And what brings you here?" Christian asked, folding his arms across his chest.

"Work." He blurted out. "I am looking for work."

Michel jingled the coins in his pocket until Christian shot him a dirty look.

"How old are you, boy?" Michel asked haughtily.

"Fourteen next month, sir."

Christian touched his head affectionately. "Where is your family?"

"Hiding in the park. We are trying to stay alive, Monsieur."

"Here, take these." He reached into his pocket and pulled out a few livres.

"Thank you, sir!" Étienne rolled the coins around his sweaty palms. "All this for me?"

"He's a rich painter, Étienne. He can afford three times what he just gave you," Michel bragged, putting his arm around the young boy.

"What do you paint?" Étienne asked, and in the moonlight Christian saw his handsome smile and full set of teeth. His eyes appeared to be a light blue. *He's a beautiful boy. Either very brave or foolish. Someone will take advantage of him, and God knows what will happen to him.*

"Portraits." Michel volunteered, pointing over his head. "He has a studio on the Rue de Rivoli."

"Have you painted the Queen?"

"No." Christian smiled.

"Now that would be something, mon ami. You and Marie Antoinette." Michel doubled over, laughing.

"And now Monsieur Forneau, we must be off." Christian nodded and shook the boy's hand. "It has been a pleasure to make your acquaintance."

"Hurry back to your family, you little runt," Michel snarled.

"Take care of yourself, Étienne." Christian smiled at the boy. Étienne thanked them profusely before running off into the darkness.

Two nights later, he showed up at Christian's studio looking for a place to sleep. Michel turned him away, but he returned the next evening and begged them again. As far as Michel was concerned, Étienne should be bled dry and his body dumped in the Bois. But Christian liked the boy; something in him touched the young vampire and reminded him of his own brother, Guillame. He missed him dearly, and so he allowed the boy to stay. Etienné never spoke of his family again. Christian wondered how they fared, and guessed that their demise was the reason Etienné had come to their door.

Étienne became their eyes and ears during the day. He managed the studio while they slept and never flinched when he learned the beautiful men who employed him were vampires. Enamored of Gabrielle and their world, he begged to be turned. So it was that two years later, at the ripe old age of sixteen, he took his last breathe as a mortal man. All he wanted was to be one of them, and Gabrielle readily obliged, taking his life and his virginity all in the same night.

Étienne had cried a river of red tears the night Christian and Michel left Paris. He had tried to warn them of the coming revolution, waving a copy of Rousseau's *The Social Contract* in their faces. As he read excerpts from it while they sat around the fireplace, Christian wondered, *why could we not see it coming?*

Michel paced like a whirling dervish. "So if he has been here for months, why is Amanda still alive?"

Christian shrugged. "I wish I knew, Michel. Whatever the reason, Gaétan is in no hurry to go home."

"Gabrielle still hates him, but sanctioned killing Amanda, yet neither she nor Étienne trusts him. No wonder they are on the verge of another civil war."

"I guess we can take comfort in the simple fact that some things never change." Christian shook his head and ran his hand through his hair. "I do know that Gaétan killed Lucien and that he took Ryan's blood for himself. It has seduced him and marred his judgment. Étienne and Gabrielle obviously suspect he killed Lucien as well, and Solange . . ."

"That is all any of us need to have happen is her coming across the Atlantic. Hey, maybe she'll kill off Gaétan and save us the mess." Michel joked as his best friend stared at the map of the Bois.

Christian feared Solange coming to New York yet deep in his heart he knew she would never face him. She would send an assassin to do her dirty work while she hid in her upscale apartment and manipulated lesser vampires. Despite Michel's confession that Gaétan fathered Solange, he could not help but still think of her as his progeny. He had spent more than one lifetime both protecting her as well as avoiding her at all costs. He needed time to ponder Étienne's phone call and speaking of phone calls. Ross had left a message but that had been over twenty-four hours ago. Where the hell was he? Everything was picking up momentum and Christian needed to sort through it all. Perhaps taking a walk and getting out of the club would help to clear his head.

Amanda left her cell phone on her lap all through dinner just in case Thomas called her. In a sense she was relieved when plans for Jeff's birthday party had changed again. He had been called out of town and would fly out early Friday morning, so Bethany had quickly changed venues and luckily everyone was able to make dinner on Thursday night instead.

Work had been tense that day and as far as Amanda knew there were no suspects in the robbery. Cole had been behind closed doors most of the day and Amanda felt like she was on automatic pilot as she tried to focus on her work. She could not wait until 5:30 had come so she could leave work.

Bethany kept giving her the "I'm so sorry" look. What she didn't understand was Amanda's sense of relief at not having to drag Thomas to the Grey Wolf later on, where Christian might also be this evening. Thomas's response—or lack thereof—had been strange, something to address when they met up again.

Amanda glanced around at all the happy couples: Bethany and Jeff, Jeff's best friend Jason and his girlfriend Marie, and Dave and Lauren. The only other person who sat alone was Charles, another close friend of Jeff's. Suddenly Amanda realized how lonely she felt. She had never imagined herself married with children; nothing about those choices appealed to her solitary, independent nature.

Jeff and Bethany would probably marry next year. They had their lives all planned out. Bethany's life seemed so easy and flawless; everything she wanted she got effortlessly. Amanda's life, meanwhile, had been one tragedy after another. That coupled with her sixth sense had given her such a strange view of the world and now she was in love with a vampire; *no infatuated with a vampire, that's different,* she told herself. It was all so weird, it was hard to believe.

"This is way cool," Jeff yelled above the music as they all entered the Grey Wolf. The group had left La Crusada and gone to another bar for drinks. After dropping off Dave and Lauren, the two couples plus Amanda and Charles entered the Grey Wolf. Bethany and Amanda feigned delight at entering such an unusual club, while Amanda kept looking for either Christian or Michel.

She tried to see who was tending the bar, but it was too crowded to even get close, but they managed to get a table in one of the side rooms. A scantily-clad young woman in black leather came out of nowhere to take their drink orders. Jeff and Bethany, along with Jason and Marie, ordered beers and then headed toward the dance floor, leaving Amanda and Charles alone.

Amanda scrambled for something to say to the prematurely balding school teacher whom she had only met once before. She decided to wait until her drink came, take a few sips, and then excuse herself to try to find either Christian or Michel. She turned her cell phone off in an act of defiance, and then she and Charles took turns yelling at each other over the music until their drinks came.

When she could not sit still any longer she politely excused herself just as her friends returned to the table. She skirted the dance floor and pushed her way over to the bar, where she saw Michel. Their eyes locked and he smiled as Amanda forced her way toward him. He came out from under the bar wearing one of his usual exotic outfits.

"Is he here tonight?" She yelled over the music.

Michel glanced around the room. "Oh, he's floating around somewhere." He smiled at her again and she suddenly felt weak, as if she were falling down a long tunnel with no end in sight. He was so dangerous looking, but she found his green eyes and sculpted face mesmerizing. She felt his power caressing her like the hands of a lover, soothing yet sensual. Amanda wondered if it was vampiric, or if he just had that much power over women. She felt the urge to run from him, unsure of his motives, just as he grabbed her hand.

She heard herself yelling in protest as he dragged her onto the crowded dance floor. She tried to protest, but it was useless. *Just one dance*, Amanda told herself. Michel led the way, pushing through the crowd and moving farther onto the dance floor. She felt sweaty; the hot lights were beating down on her and the loud music pounding her body. Her uncomfortable shoes made it hard for her to dance. Michel wrapped his long arms around her shoulders. It felt too intimate for her, but before she could react he pulled her toward him.

She focused on his chest, which was adorned with silver necklaces. He let her go and held his arms over his head, dancing around her like a flame, hot and intense. Out of the corner of her eye, she noticed people staring at the beautiful vampire writhing under the warm lights, barely sweating. His hair swirled around his stunning face. His carefree demeanor felt liberating to her, and suddenly, she didn't care what anyone thought. She was enamored by him and found herself dancing in his arms, spinning frantically, laughing, and letting herself go.

Whether she was releasing the stress of the day or had fallen under his spell, she didn't care. He rubbed himself up against her and she laughed; she spun in his arms, pressed her back up against his chest, and gyrated into him while he held on to her. She tossed her head back and laughed at the irony of dancing with one beautiful vampire while wanting his best friend.

Christian called Ross again, but the phone just rang. When he got voice mail he hung up. *Where is he tonight?* He tried calling Ross's direct line at the precinct, but again he got his voice mail. He would give him until tomorrow night to call him back. In total frustration, he shoved his cell phone in his pants pocket, and headed out down a long hallway out the back door. He had just left the bar when he realized that he forgot to tell Michel something important. As he charged in through the back entrance toward the dance floor he stopped.

Amanda's here.

He came to a dead halt and scanned the room; her presence filled his senses. She was close by, and Michel was not behind the bar. He stormed toward the dance floor and then stopped; his best friend was laughing and dancing with the object of his desire. He felt a burst of jealousy, mesmerized by the sight of Michel and Amanda moving as one under the hot lights. He could see her clearly through the crowd; her short dress, black stockings, and stiletto heels driving him wild. Christian imagined them wrapped around him. She wore little makeup, only dark red lipstick and her hair was wild.

What is she doing here?

She looked so beautiful. She was petite; dark. She was exactly the type of women that attracted him and kept turning up in his fantasies; only she was real, and she was here again. *How many times can our paths cross before I can no longer resist her?* Christian read Michel's face and his message. *If you want her, come and take her away from me.* He watched as she twirled around Michel, and was reminded of the earlier confession Michel had made to Christian about Josette and Gaétan. Had she really had another affair with him or was Michel Solange's father? He thought that Gabrielle had been the only woman they had shared, yet despite their centuries of friendship, something had always gnawed at him. Watching Michel dance with Amanda made him wonder about Michel's motives with the young beauty. Folding his arms across his chest, he leaned up against the bar.

"What are you waiting for?" Sabin asked him.

Amanda felt a tap on her shoulder and turned to find Bethany and Jeff dancing close by. Jeff smiled and eyed Michel suspiciously; Bethany ignored Michel completely, as if they had never met. Michel gave no indication that he knew her, either. When a tall brunette had wedged herself between Amanda and Michel, she took it as her cue to get off the dance floor. *Even if he is here, why would I risk being rejected again? I can't handle any more conversations with Charles. Maybe it's just time to go home.*

She turned her back on Michel and began to push her way back toward their table when someone grabbed her hand. For a second she thought it was Bethany trying to get her attention again. She turned into a pair of dark eyes that took her breath away. He wore the same shredded shirt she had seen him in once before, only this time he wore dark jeans. As he bent down to whisper in her ear, his hair brushed past her shoulder and Amanda thought she would faint.

"So were you going to leave without introducing all of us?"

"I was a little distracted by Michel."

"He has that affect on women." He tried to smile. "Are you okay, Amanda? You don't look well."

"Not really . . . it's been a rough few days and I think it's all caught up with me. I didn't want to come here. Plans changed and . . . I'd better get going." She blurted it out without thinking, fearful of being rejected by him again, especially if that beautiful brunette was anywhere close by.

"Let's go where it is quiet so we can talk."

"Are you alone?" She asked meeting his gaze.

"Yes, I am."

Before she could protest, she felt a cool hand on her back. He ushered her through the crowd and down a familiar dark hallway. Opening the office door, he moved aside letting her enter first.

"Sit down." He gestured toward the leather couch. She sat at the far end of the couch.

"The museum was robbed on Tuesday morning." She blurted out. She waited for a reaction but got none. *Did he know something about it?*

As she filled him in on the details, she tried to gauge his reaction, although she was not sure exactly why. Something told her he knew more than he was letting on. Perhaps it was tied into her suspicion that he and Ross were more than casual acquaintances. It was nothing she could prove, just something that she felt, and she never doubted her gut instincts.

"I was shocked when Cole told me that there was nothing caught on tape. How can that be, Christian? It just doesn't make sense."

"I don't know, Amanda. Professionals have all sorts of ways of stealing things." He picked up a strand of his hair and began to twirl it around his finger.

"That's just it. The stolen object was beautiful, don't get me wrong, but my god, if you are going to steal from the Met, there are so many objects in those galleries alone that are more valuable. It's like the robbery was secondary to something else."

"It sounds like a police matter. Anyone possibly involved will be questioned, and if I know Detective Ross, he will be thorough. What is it, Amanda?"

"Since that night in the tunnel last summer, my life has been a roller coaster of strange events with no resolution. You told me at your house the other night that I needed to trust you, and that you needed to keep hiding things from me in order to keep me out of danger. That doesn't seem fair, does it?"

"Lots of things in life aren't fair Amanda. The fact that you are alone without your special man; now that seems quite unfair to me. Where is he tonight?"

Amanda jumped up off the couch but he beat her to the door.

"I am sorry," he whispered. "That was uncalled for."

She wanted to move but she was lost in his eyes.

"Please stay," he heard himself ask before he could stop himself. He reached down and gently caressed her cheek.

Amanda felt a jolt run through her body. Mesmerized by his eyes, his face, she could not move away.

"Every time we meet, you either dismiss me or I run away. Now I understand, after meeting Eve the other night. I . . . I didn't know that you had someone special—"

Amanda painfully reminded him of being young and vulnerable. She seemed angry at the world, which he understood, and constantly denied her need for people. She reminded him that human suffering was timeless, something that hundreds of years and immortal powers could not abate. The feeling of an eternal emptiness, of knowing he was only temporarily sating a need that could never be satisfied by sex or blood alone. The instincts of being immortal ruled him, but a nameless, faceless emptiness filled him up and twisted his stomach into knots.

He had tried to speak to Gabrielle about it when they had first become lovers, before La Révolution Française. He often brought it up to her when they were alone, lying in the darkness after a night of hunting and making love. The only counsel she could offer him was to remain her lover. Once he had met Josette and had fallen in love with her, she eased the emptiness and dark despair of his endless existence. Perhaps it was something Gabrielle did not feel, or never wanted to admit to him.

Amanda tried to get past him again.

"I better go Christian."

"Just hold still and let me love you." He begged as he pulled her close. "Come home with me," he whispered into her ear. "I may be immortal, but there's still a man underneath. You have to believe that."

Chapter Twenty-One

❦

CENTRAL PARK WAS blanketed in snow. Gaétan came down the hill out of the Ramble and headed south toward Bethesda Fountain. He thought the snow-covered trees reflected in the clear, still lake were beautiful. Nothing stirred; his footsteps made no sound. He still felt restless and agitated, even after having killed Ross. Was the blood changing him? It felt as though his vampire nature was melding with his once mortal coil, which he could barely remember existing.

It was as if there were two distinct energies inside of him. The vampire he was and the stranger he was becoming, as though his life were meaningless, a void broken up by the kill. He felt detached from a power that had been his for over five hundred years. His pulsating energy felt muted, like a watercolor painting left out in a rainstorm. The colors were there but the image was indistinguishable. Solange, Gabrielle, and Paris felt far away and foreign, like a previous lifetime half remembered through dreams.

Solange was begging him to come back home to her, but where was home? He no longer felt any connection to Paris, to his apartment, or her. He suddenly felt weary and old; used up by the very blood he thought would give him life.

He found himself walking down Fifth Avenue across from E. 83rd street. Just then a cab stopped and two people emerged. Gaétan froze as a familiar silhouette, clothed in a long dark coat held the door of the cab for a woman he recognized. Gaétan came closer as Christian shut the cab door and grabbed Amanda's hand. Leading her up the stairs, he glanced behind him as if he sensed an intruder nearby. Then the door shut as Gaétan hid in the shadows across the street.

A light on the first floor illuminated the otherwise dark mansion then another light on the third floor went on. Gaétan thought he would be furious, unable to contain his own rage at the enemy that had stolen Josette away from him all those centuries ago and now had Amanda, but he felt nothing. It was as if he were watching someone else's life not his own.

Amanda took a deep breath and followed Christian up carpeted steps and past the beautiful paintings in the foyer. She was barely able to keep up with him in the darkness. He led her through a set of French doors into a large living room. The room was clearly a testament to Christian's love of books and antiques. It felt strangely familiar to her, like a dream remembered hours after waking.

In the center of the room two floral couches sat opposite each other. The wall to the left held floor-to-ceiling book cases. On the right was a large, black marble fireplace with a black marble bust on each end to give it symmetry. A gilded mirror covered the entire wall behind the fireplace, ending at the twelve-foot ceilings.

As her eyes adjusted, she noticed more busts and antique tables set throughout the room. A beautiful glass vase with a bouquet of fresh flowers rested on a coffee table. It gave the room a cozy feel and brought it into the present day. She wandered passed him to what looked like an original Hepplewhite game table and four chairs. Stacks of books covered the tabletop. She stopped at the French windows.

"Do you go for walks in the park?"

"Almost every night." He approached her slowly.

"God, it must be so beautiful, especially Bethesda Terrace. That's the most magical place."

"You should see it on a summer night at about three AM with the moon shining down on the water," he confessed, leaning up against the window frame beside her.

"I can't even imagine it." Amanda shook her head, thinking aloud.

She glanced around the room at the beautiful furnishings and books, and suddenly her life felt so banal and dull. "Your house is equally as beautiful. What a world you have here."

Amanda dared to glance at him. Her mind raced through the events of the past few weeks to this moment. *How did I get here?* She felt the adrenaline rush through her, and although she wasn't a night person, she guessed it was most likely responsible for keeping her so awake.

"You are welcome to my world, Amanda; to as much or as little as you would like from me." His voice wrapped around her, his confession stunning her.

"What are you trying to say?"

She felt the pull of his dark sensual eyes.

He brushed her hair away from her face. "Whatever you want from me is yours, except immortality."

He felt like a dream to her, and now he was saying things that only happened in fantasies. She could barely get the words out. "Everything has a price. What is yours?"

"My price is trust; your trust."

"Trust is built over time and you can't rush it. You of all people should know that." She folded her arms across her chest, suddenly feeling cold.

"That is true, but time can also be a curse, Amanda. You can't imagine looking backward, watching the world change as you try to adapt. Most of us go mad after a century or so, after everyone we love is gone. Our very existence no longer seems relevant to anything."

She sensed that the world he had created here was what he missed most, his life in eighteenth-century France, which happened to be the time period she loved more than any other in history. The coincidences were startling. *But there are no coincidences, Amanda, remember?*

"You told me that you always saw me as your protector, your guardian angel. Let me love and protect you."

"What are you trying to protect me from, Christian?"

He pulled her close again. "Later, Amanda, please just stay here with me tonight."

She smiled then he took her hand and led her back through the elegant living room out into the hallway. Turning left, they went up another flight of stairs. The air felt warmer and smelled of smoke. He opened a door and she followed him, entering a room bathed in firelight.

She stopped just inside the door, feeling as though she had stepped into one of the period rooms in the museum.

"This is *your* bedroom?"

His bedroom reflected an eighteenth-century sensibility with a few twenty-first-century touches such as blinds on the windows and a portable phone. The Louis XVI furniture reflected the daintiness of the times, but instead of being painted with gold ormolu, all his furniture was Beachwood. *Not light, but not quite dark, either, like his hair.*

The focus of the room was a king-size bed that stood to her right, opposite a large armoire that covered the entire opposite wall. Covered with lace pillows and a lace coverlet, the bed looked sensual, yet cozy. At the foot of his bed was a matching loveseat. A lace canopy jutted out from the ten-foot ceiling, and an overstuffed chair completed the room.

"Who's your decorator?" She joked, deciding his room was not too feminine. She found herself wandering around and imagined waking up here every morning beside him. Noticing the heavy blinds, she was reminded that he never saw the sun. As she took in the room, Amanda was inexplicably drawn to a tiny painting above the fireplace. Looking at the portrait, she forgot all about his furniture. A young, dark-haired woman gazed longingly out from the painting. She wore a luxurious, low-cut green silk gown that matched her eyes. Her curly brown hair was piled high on her head and framed a heart-shaped face with high cheekbones. But it was her smile that captivated Amanda; it reminded her of someone, but who?

Christian remembered the summer night that Luc Delacore walked into his studio. He had wanted to give his young bride a portrait for her birthday, only months away. He made all the arrangements through Étienne. The next evening she came to Christian's studio with a young couple. Étienne welcomed them and offered them wine and cheese. Christian could hear his young servant entertaining them while he prepared the sitting area for the beautiful mortal.

His patron was not an old man who had married a child bride, but he was probably thirty years old, which in 1787 made him old. Josette was no more than fifteen. Delacore's first wife had died from the pox, which loomed forever as a threat to the city. Christian was especially sensitive about it since it had killed his mother when he was a child.

Christian swaggered into the room full of mortals, and there she stood; his dark beauty with green eyes and a beautiful smile. She extended her hand as if they had only just met, though they had been lovers for some time. He took it cautiously, kissing it gently, and they both laughed at their deception.

"She's beautiful." Amanda studied the painting closer. "Who was the artist?"

"Me," he smugly replied. "I had a studio in Paris for several years."

"You are really talented. What was her name?"

"Josette. Josette Delacore."

"Who was she?"

"She was the young wife of a nobleman." Amanda gently ran her fingertips along the edge of the frame, as images flooded her.

❦

The knot was too tight. Amanda watched the blindfolded woman trying to wriggle free. Kneeling, with her hands tied behind her, she could barely keep her balance in the center of the canopied bed. Amanda felt as if she were in the room, somehow inside the woman's head, reliving the memory with her. The lit candelabra cast the room in long shadows, and the sweet-smelling wax masked the scent of dung and sewage. Amanda watched as the woman struggled, her black corset a dramatic contrast against her milky white skin. Her thick dark hair, piled high off her neck.

An open window against a dark sky let in all sorts of sounds from the street below: laughter, a town crier, horses and carriages clomping on dirt. Amanda could feel the woman's heart racing. Was it in anticipation, or fear? Out of the shadows, a man slunk gracefully onto the bed behind her, like a cat. He appeared to be dressed only in trousers.

The women muttered something in French, her accent heavy. He ran his hands down her spine and up her rib cage. She lost her balance and pitched forward, but he grabbed her, murmuring into her hair.

"We do not have much time." He whispered into her hair as he kissed her neck.

Amanda thought she recognized his voice, but no, it could not be.

The woman pressed up against him as he grabbed her from behind and bent over her neck. She threw back her head in ecstasy and gasped as a thin rivulet of blood ran down her neck between her breasts.

Moments later he released her and circled around to face her. It was then that Amanda saw his face and felt herself shutter. Thomas? No, it could not be, yet he had the same hair and smile, even down to his dimples. She tried to imagine him in modern clothing.

"Please, Gaétan," the woman begged. "Please, untie me."

"Of course, my Josette."

Voices were as distinct as fingerprints. Amanda knew it was Thomas, and then the realization came to her. He was immortal.

And I have slept with him too.

Amanda backed away from the painting trying to make sense of the images.

"Amanda, what is it?" Christian asked, taken aback by her reaction.

"Nothing . . . I sometimes get these flashes when I touch things . . . it's as if I see things…. like a film strip running in my head."

He rubbed her shoulder.

"The man she was with, Gaétan…it's weird but he looks and sounds just like my friend Thomas from the Met?"

Christian sat down on his bed, his worst fear realized.

"I'm sorry to blow you away . . . I don't know how I do it, but I have this gift."

Christian ran his hand through his hair.

"What was she like?" Amanda asked, almost afraid to ask anything else about the mysterious Josette Delacore.

He tried to smile. "She reminds me of you."

"Bookish, a loner?" She said, trying to make a joke to lighten the mood.

"No. Intelligent, kind, strong-willed, curious." He reached up and gently brushed his fingers along her face. "Spellbindingly beautiful and unique."

Amanda swooned at his touch and felt her breath catch in her throat. She could not look away as the adrenaline rushed through her.

"Did you share her?" She asked, her curiosity getting the better of her.

"She had a husband as well."

"Was his name Gaétan?" She asked impulsively, thinking that perhaps he was her husband and Christian her lover.

"No, Luc Delacore. Josette had other lovers as well as a husband."

His words sounded icy and Amanda wondered how he could tolerate such infidelity from someone he obviously loved so deeply.

"How could any woman want more than you?" She smiled and kissed his cold cheek, afraid to ask him anymore questions.

She lifted the black sheer shift up over her head and dropped it on the bed. Christian remained motionless, watching her.

"Unzip me," she commanded, turning around. She felt his cold fingers trace the smooth lines of her neck as he slowly unzipped her dress. She stared down at the oriental carpet and tried to control her heartbeat. She felt the back of her dress open and a rush of arousal flow through her body. She turned slowly and met his eyes, holding her dress up at her shoulders.

I want him as I have wanted nothing else in my life. Let him have you. Don't look back, Amanda.

She felt the dress brush her legs on its way to the floor which left her standing in her black underwear.

"Turn around. Let me look at you." He seemed to smile with his eyes.

She liked the feeling of him devouring her with his eyes and she forgot about Thomas and the robbery at the museum. Nothing had prepared her for him. He was all she could think about, and for him she would toss her judgment to the wind. In one fluid vampiric motion, he bent down to pick up her dress as she stepped out of it. He tossed it on the chair before sitting back down in front of her on the bed.

"I would never hurt you, Amanda, despite what I am."

"I know that, just as I know there is no turning back after tonight."

He leaned over and ran his hands up her legs.

"Tonight is only the beginning."

PART FOUR

Chapter Twenty-Two

GAÉTAN LEAPT EFFORTLESSLY onto the townhouse roof, remembering a summer night in Paris long after Josette had left him for Christian. He had had other lovers, but Josette had always been special, and he had never forgotten her. She still shared the royal apartment with her husband, Luc, but Christian and Michel were fixtures there, and in the halls of the lesser French nobility.

Gaétan recalled staring up at Josette's bedroom window and then jumping onto her roof, wondering who was inside and what was happening between them. He remembered seeing Josette wrapped around the eternally beautiful Michel and laughing to himself, thinking that it served Christian right.

Gaétan wondered if Christian had ever known that he was being cuckolded by his best friend. And then there was Luc Delacore, who probably had no idea his wife had been the lover of not one but three vampires. When the child came, he wondered which one of them had fathered her, but as Solange grew, he saw the resemblance to Michel.

How could Christian not see it too?

Now, gently pressing his face up to the glass, his mouth dropped in amazement. He could feel their desire for each other as if it were a tangible thing, ready to burst throughout the room. He watched Christian lying on his bed as Amanda crawled toward him on her knees. His dark eyes never left her face; he reminded Gaétan of a dying man in a desert, looking at a cup of water.

"What are you doing?" Christian whispered, trying to sit up on the bed. He was always the one to take the initiative with his conquests. It aroused him to seduce them while he controlled them.

She crawled on top of him.

"I want to make love to you. Just lie still," she whispered, kissing his face and his neck.

"You're so beautiful," the vampire gasped. He had wanted her for so long and finally she was here with him. It felt surreal. Amanda's heartbeat soothed him yet he fought the scent of her blood.

As they kissed more passionately, the temptation to take her blood began to cloud his judgment. He told himself that if he tasted her he was no better than Solange or Gaétan in wanting her for their own gains. He loved her and was sworn to protect her. How could he take something from her now, something so powerful yet so forbidden?

Christian tried to clear his head, but he could not fight his lust for her and the pounding of her blood in his head. Pulling her closer on top of him, he felt his own release as he bit into her warm flesh. She moaned as he held her like a child, a trusting child who would die if he did not release her.

At first Christian felt nothing and suddenly it was as if molten lava were coursing through his veins. As he held on to Amanda, the room began to spin. His stomach knotted as something ever so subtle began to happen. Memories of his childhood, his mother, and his youth filled his head. Poignant memories of being mortal—times long forgotten—collided against the vampire he had been for centuries and then melded into one. He was swept away by a euphoria he had never experienced before and did not want to lose.

It's the blood talking, making me feel my mortal life again.

He ran his hand up her warm body and willed himself to let go of her.

Amanda fell onto the lace blanket, her body pale and glistening with sweat as blood ran down her chest. Her beautiful eyes glazed over as he licked the wounds until they closed over then put the heavy blanket around her.

The townhouse was still, with only the occasional sound of a car passing by to break the silence. The wall sconce lighting was low, leaving most of the living room in shadows. Christian lay sprawled out on the couch in only his jeans, trying to focus on a Stephen King novel; he turned the pages so rapidly that it appeared he was only pretending to read, yet he devoured each word. He had left Amanda upstairs in his room asleep.

Dawn was coming, and for the first time in decades he wished he could push back the sunrise so he could stay with her. After coming downstairs, he had checked his cell phone. He found no more messages from Ross, and the creeping feeling inside him began to

191

turn into panic. Had something happened to the detective? The door opened silently and Michel slipped in, closing it behind him. He sat on the couch across from Christian, crossed one long leg over another, and began to absentmindedly drum his fingers on his boots.

"What is it, Michel?" Christian asked, trying to ignore him. Michel slipped off the chair and slunk over to the windows to peer out into the darkness.

"Nothing," Michel waved and wandered back to the Hepplewhite table. He attempted to grab a book off the stack, but it slipped out of his hands and crashed onto the table, toppling the rest of the books.

"Merde!" He bent down, picked up the scattered books, and tried to straighten up the piles.

"Would you please sit down?" Christian tried not to raise his voice as he took his eyes from the page.

Michel sauntered back to the chair and sat down again. Christian could sense his agitation. Finally he set his book down.

"So how was the club?"

Michel shrugged. "Oh, you know, the usual coeds and all."

Christian watched his best friend trying to feign lightheartedness, but he knew Michel was as rattled as he was over Étienne's disturbing phone call. Making love to Amanda had taken his mind off it only briefly.

"So how was it?"

"It?"

"Come on." Michel smiled. "You have been pining away for this mortal for years now. Was she everything you imagined her to be?"

"All that and more," Christian confessed, trying not to smile.

"And you were not tempted by her blood?"

Older vampires needed less blood. It was as if age brought a cessation to the cravings, and at nearly three hundred years old, he and Michel could sustain themselves on very little. He could not bear to tell his friend how Amanda's blood had called to him and how he had given in; unable to control himself.

"I managed to suppress it, Michel." He picked up a strand of his hair and began to twirl it around his finger. "If I didn't, I would be no better than our Parisian friends."

Michel nodded, and Christian thought he seemed distracted and far away.

"Look, I know hearing from Étienne was startling to say the least, but it was good to hear his voice again." He tried to sound jovial. "I have not heard from Ross, and I am getting worried for him."

Michel brought his knees up to his chest and wrapped his arms around them.

"They are coming. I can feel it."

Michel's seriousness and honesty made Christian's stomach flip. His usual joking had been replaced by sheer terror. He was scared, almost curled up in a ball on the couch.

"Michel, you have to have faith in us. We can beat them."

"I felt something near the house tonight. Maybe it's my paranoia," Michel stammered. "I don't know, mon ami." He ran his hand through his hair, then got up and went to the window. "Don't you ever wonder if this life has just gotten old and stale? When suddenly faced with my possible demise, I can't think of one thing that I would miss, except you. Perhaps it is time—"

Christian sat up in a panic. "What are you saying, Michel?"

"That I have lived long enough. Amanda is different, Christian. I see how much you love her. Usually with mortals, their minds cannot comprehend what we are. Oh, they are dazzled by our looks and our power, but their minds cannot truly comprehend our essence. She knows what we are yet she accepts us and she still wants you...just like Josette."

"It is you who can't stay away from them," Christian reminded him. Christian thought Michel seemed unusually philosophical this morning.

"They love the idea of the cinematic vampire, but not the real thing, you know?"

What is the real thing, Michel? Please tell me, for I fear I do not know anymore.

"I don't understand, Michel. Sex is the only thing you have ever wanted from mortals; to seduce and then discard them."

"Seduction is the only thing I can want. There can be nothing more."

Christian shook his head. "You have never allowed there to be anything more."

"I hate to quote her, but Gabrielle always said mortals and vampires don't mix. It always turns out badly. Josette was taken away from you. You don't know how much longer it would have gone on, Christian."

Since it seemed to be the night of true confessions, Christian thought he should ask his closest friend if he had slept with Josette or had been in love with her, but he could not bring himself to ask Michel. *Suppose he said yes, then what?*

"I suppose I will never know if another vampire would have stolen her from me."

Michel chuckled. Christian thought it sounded tin-like and hollow in the quiet room. Christian recognized that laughter. All of their kind seemed to acquire it. It happened when their minds finally wrapped around the notion of eternity and the loneliness that became a bitter companion forever.

Christian headed upstairs to check on Amanda one more time. She was wrapped up under the covers, bathed in the predawn light. It felt so odd to have her here in his bed. *How I wish I could curl up next to her.* He sat down on the bed and touched her as if she were made of porcelain and would break.

Her eyes fluttered open. "What time is it?"

"Five AM. Time for all good vampires to go to sleep."

"You look so serious. What's wrong?"

"It's almost dawn, Amanda. We'll talk tomorrow night."

'What is tomorrow, Friday?"

He nodded. She grabbed his cold hand. "Why can't you stay here? What happens to you?"

How could he explain how the darkness came, pushing all thoughts away from him until he just fell into a void that claimed him every day.

He shrugged, his face remaining expressionless. "I die every day. Sometimes I dream, but usually it's like I am sucked into a black hole devoid of all color or light. Then I wake once the sun sets."

The room smelled of sweat and sex, and all he wanted to do was to hold her. It was something he had not done since he was a mortal man. Christian had all but forgotten the comfort of sleeping beside someone.

He held her close to him and whispered in her hair, "I have to go, Amanda."

"Hurry back," she whispered.

Christian quietly shut his bedroom door, only to find Michel hovering there.

"I think you need to come up to the roof."

Once upstairs Christian sniffed the cold air and headed over to the ledge overlooking Fifth Avenue.

"Gaétan?" Michel asked, staying near the door to the roof. "How could he know where we live?"

"I don't know." Christian closed his eyes as the warm rays of the sun called to him. *Perhaps I can just stay here and see the sunrise. Oh God, to be mortal again, if only for one day.*

Michel grabbed him. "What are you doing? The sun is coming up!"

His best friend dragged him inside just as the sun hit the top of the building.

Chapter Twenty-Three

❦

THE AROMA OF coffee stirred her yet it took a moment to remember where she was and the night before. Rustling at the foot of the bed alarmed her enough to peek out from the covers.

"Good afternoon," Tony quipped, setting down a steaming carafe of coffee.

She tried to sit up, but felt dizzy. Then she remembered that she was naked and buried herself under the covers again.

"Why are you being so nice to me?" Amanda asked and noticed a vase full of white roses and a card on the night table.

"Under orders," he snapped. "There's cream, sugar and some pastries."

"All my favorites," she replied, studying the tray. The room was awash in muted sunlight. "What time is it?"

"Oh, around two in the afternoon," he replied, staying near the foot of the bed. "There are some sweaters and jeans over here. Size six foot I presume? Christian asked me to bring some stuff in here for you. He said you couldn't go home in what you wore last night. It got pretty trashed."

Amanda felt herself blush as bits and pieces of the night before began to reform in her mind. She decided that Tony was not going to win at whatever game they were playing and so she tried to hold the covers against her chest and sit up at the same time.

"The bathroom's right through there." He pointed behind him. "Stay as long as you like. I'm here until sundown if you need anything."

"Where's Christian? I mean I know he's—"

"Come on, I can't tell you that." He shrugged as he rolled his eyes. "He asked that you meet him on the museum steps around nine tonight."

Amanda had to think for a moment what day it was; the last few days had begun to meld into one. Thank goodness she had requested this Friday off. She reminded Cole she was always available by phone in case he needed her. She reached up to brush the hair off her face and felt something on her neck. She noticed Tony watching her.

"Okay." She glanced at her fingertips, not sure what she was looking for, but feeling something there nonetheless. "Thanks for everything, Tony."

She thought he smiled as he raced for the door. "I'm here if you need me."

Once she was sure he was gone, Amanda jumped out of bed and poured herself a cup of coffee in what looked like eighteenth-century china, checked her cell phone for messages, found none and made her way to the bathroom to clean up. The black-and-white floor tiles felt cold on her bare feet. She grabbed the cup of coffee making her way to the bathroom. Most of the room was taken up by a large sunken bathtub lined with bottles of shampoo and various other toiletries. Dark wooden cabinets and a double sink took up another wall. Black towels hung on a brass towel rack, and the typical low lighting, which she was slowly growing accustomed to, gave the room a cozy glow.

Amanda flipped on the tub's water faucets and tossed in something grainy that smelled great. She guessed it was bath salts, but she was unable to translate the French label. Checking out her neck in the mirror, Amanda noticed two tiny marks on the left side. Memories of making love to Christian flooded her. The experience was ineffable, and when he bit her neck, she had lost all control. His lovemaking felt like a wave, moving slowly over them both, engulfing her in its power. She needed to feel his eyes on her and his touch. He made her feel like the most loved woman in the world. She wondered if that was his supernatural powers talking or actual love and desire.

Amanda remembered whispering to him that she loved him. Was that so wrong? She told herself to not think about the future, but rather to enjoy the now, yet she knew they were fated to be together. How could that be possible? As she stepped into the tub, she wondered where he and Michel slept. Was he close by? A million thoughts raced through her head as she soaked in the warm water. What was happening with the robbery? What would happen between them now that she had fallen so in love with him? Tony had mentioned there were clothes for her, but how had Christian known she wore a size six shoe? Amanda submerged herself in the sudsy water, feeling special in this different world.

She wondered how the rest of the evening had gone for Bethany and Jeff, and where Thomas had disappeared to. Though he had not called her back, she could not imagine he wanted her just for sex. They had been friends, and though he was a great lover, he paled after her night with Christian. She washed her hair with something that smelled like grapefruit, and then grabbed one of the thick black bath towels. After putting on a body lotion that smelled like lavender, Amanda went to find some clothes.

She rummaged through the neatly stacked jeans, shirts, and sweaters, but she could not decide what to wear. *How could he know my tastes?* She settled on a pair of black jeans, a white boat neck sweater, and a short gray woolen jacket. He had socks, underclothes, and several pairs of boots for her as well. She got dressed quickly, and then went back into the bathroom to blow dry her hair. Glancing at her watch, she saw that it was after three. She checked her messages and decided to call Bethany and check in with her. While she was dialing, she remembered the card accompanying the flowers. The call went into voice mail, and she left a brief message.

"Hey, Beth, it's me. It's around three o'clock on Friday afternoon. I . . . I spent the night with Christian. I'm on my way home. See you later."

She hung up and opened the small card beside the flowers. In neat black ink was the following:

My Amanda,
I am at a loss for words.
My heart beats only for you and love runs through my veins.

C

Amanda sniffed the roses and noticed that there was one lily in the bouquet. *How does he know this is my favorite flower?* The meaning of the lily, *I dare you to love me*— was not lost on her. He had offered her everything, including an invitation into his world, and at that moment it all seemed possible and perfectly rational—Yet he was a vampire, a blood drinker who was nearly three hundred years old. As she ate a chocolate croissant and drank another cup of coffee, Amanda pondered his presence in her life. Clearly he knew everything about her, but why? And what kind of future could they possibly have together? When she finished her breakfast, she forced herself to leave.

She stopped before the portrait over the fireplace one more time, curious about this woman who had so captured his heart that he still could not let her go centuries later. *How can I compete with her?* She was tempted to touch the painting again, but then thought better of it. It was time to go back to her post WWII apartment and her average life. Fearing the flowers would not survive the return trip in the cold air, she left them in the vase on the night table. Taking a pen out of her purse, she turned the card over and scribbled a quick note to him.

I double dare you . . . Amanda

With her purse over her shoulder, Amanda tiptoed down the steps. She stopped in front of the French doors to confirm that the living room was just as beautiful as she remembered it. She opened the doors and slipped into the elegant room. The furniture and antiques appeared muted in the late afternoon sun. Amanda walked over to a window and glanced down at the traffic on Fifth Avenue and the museum that was her world. *Can I have both?* She slowly buttoned her coat and headed downstairs, hesitant to trade this sanctuary for the cold New York City afternoon.

On her way out, she stuck her head in the library to thank Tony, but her attention was drawn to something on the mantle. She approached it carefully, feeling as though she were hallucinating. Was it one of his valuable antiques, or no, it could not be? She hesitated at first, thinking it merely a coincidence that he would have a terra cotta statue on his mantle. Amanda tried to remember if it had been there the other night.

There's only one way to find out, Amanda. Turn it over.

She tiptoed over to the mantle just as Tony came in behind her. A rush of images hit her: a feminine bedroom with blue walls, a chandelier filled with candlelight, a woman's laughter.

"Did you find everything okay?"

She debated whether there was enough time to turn the statue over and look for an accession number.

"Yes. I was just admiring this sculpture. It's beautiful."

He came up beside her, and his amber eyes met her gaze. "I never noticed it before. He sure does love his antiques."

She set it back down on the mantle, willing her hands not to shake.

"Thanks for everything, Tony." She smiled, trying to get beyond his cold façade.

"Just doing my job," he smiled and followed her back to the foyer.

Amanda kicked herself all the way home for not turning the statue over while she had the chance. *Was I not fast enough, or did I just not want to know the truth?* She turned the key in the lock of her apartment and stepped inside. As she hung up the rich woolen jacket, she surveyed her apartment. It suddenly felt jejune compared to where she had just spent the night.

She had just gotten online when she heard the front door open.

"Amanda?"

Her bedroom door opened and Bethany stuck her head in. She looked refreshed, dressed entirely in black with her hair pulled back in a ponytail. "Are you just getting home?"

"Didn't you get my message?"

Bethany sat down on her bed hesitantly. "What's going on, Amanda? You don't have a date in over a year, and within the space of three days you sleep with two different guys?"

"I don't know . . . It just happened, Beth." She ran her hand through her hair, wondering the same thing herself.

"Nice clothes."

How could she explain that a vampire just happened to know her shoe size and her favorite brand of clothing? None of it made sense. It was like he knew everything about her. She had never withheld anything from Bethany, yet now she was privy to a secret world, one that most people did not believe existed. How could she tell her the truth?

"Amanda, look, I know this last year has been really rough. I can't even imagine what you must have gone through. I never doubted your story ..." she shrugged and smiled at Amanda. "Okay, I had a hard time believing that vampire's killed Ryan and a guy with a machete saved your life. But you proved me wrong about him. He does exist. I guess what I am trying to say is, who am I to judge you? I happen to like Thomas, but if you want to sleep around, hey, just practice safe sex."

Amanda realized she had not used birth control with either of them. It was not like her to get swept up in the moment, but with both of them the experience had bordered on mystical.

"Thanks, Beth. So how did Jeff like the Grey Wolf?"

She shrugged. "He was so drunk by that point I'm not sure if he even remembered going there, but it was a nice party, don't you think?"

"It was great." Amanda smiled. "You two seem so happy."

"There's something you're not telling me, Amanda Monique Perretti." Like Amanda's mother, Bethany only used her full name to denote a serious tone to any conversation.

"You need to sit down Beth, there's something—"

Cole was on the line. Amanda flipped open her cell phone.

"Hi, Amanda. I'm glad I caught you at home. Have you seen the news today?" She put her hand over the receiver. "Beth, put on the TV."

Bethany ran into the living room with Amanda close behind.

Staring at the two women from the television screen was a photo of Detective Burt Ross and footage of his hysterical girlfriend, Melinda.

Amanda held her cell phone by her ear as the three of them watched the story.

"He's wanted for questioning Amanda. NYPD are looking at him as a possible suspect."

Chapter Twenty-Four

❧

SOLANGE ROLLED OVER in the darkness into the arms of her newest lover, Augustin. He was a powerful vampire for one so young. At only one hundred years old, he had acquired a reputation for being dangerous and extremely arrogant, qualities she needed in a lover and admired in a companion. He reminded her of Gaétan in many ways, yet he was more ruthless, bordering on vicious. Solange needed Augustin. He loved making her happy, not just in bed but anywhere else they managed to find themselves, too. He was a skilled hunter, and they would wander in the Bois together for hours, making a game out of stalking prostitutes before killing them savagely. She studied his protruding jaw, heavy-lidded dark eyes, and dirty blond hair. His face appeared softer than usual, an indication that he had good news.

He touched her cold face and ran his hand over her high cheekbones as she smiled coyly up at him.

"We take him tonight, just before dawn." His deep voice filled the bedroom and Solange began to tremble with excitement.

"Are you sure Gabrielle has no idea about this, Augustin?" She brushed his hair away from his face.

They had been preparing for weeks now, waiting for the right moment to attack the illustrious vampires. Solange was not sure of the exact moment she had realized that Gaétan might never return to her. Augustin had tried to convince her that he was either dead or had fallen for the young mortal and chosen to remain in New York. At first Solange dismissed his accusations, calling him jealous and petty but lately she had begun to accept it. She and Augustin had an understanding; he would never replace Gaétan. When the older vampire returned, Augustin would leave her bed willingly; but they were spending every night together now, and she began to see herself as his only lover.

Their plan was two-fold, and they rehashed it constantly after being sated with blood and love-making; kill both Gabrielle and Étienne, and with the older ones dead they could rule Paris together. At first Solange had not thought it possible, but her spies had recently informed her that the two ancient lovers had parted. Gabrielle had retained her apartment, while Étienne had returned to the catacombs. All Augustin needed was the right opportunity to strike, and the rest would be easy.

"It is as I told you, Solange," he whispered. "They are no longer together. The stupid mortals I hired will drag him away just as he falls asleep and chain him in the Bois. When the sun rises, he will die a slow death in the winter sun."

Solange giggled and sat up, naked. "What about that bitch?"

"Have no fear. She will be taken as well, just as the sun rises. She won't know what hit her until it is too late. They can watch each other die."

Solange jumped up out of bed. "If this works, there is nothing stopping us."

She kissed his chest slowly. "I need food, Augustin."

"I have a surprise for you."

Solange waited alone in the dark and then the smell hit her. A mortal was in the house. As the scent grew stronger, Augustin came closer with a tiny woman pressed up against him. Solange knew by her eyes that Augustin had hypnotized her, rendering her weak and disoriented. She was dressed entirely in leather; her dark eye makeup ran down her cheeks from her tears.

"Isn't she just lovely, Augustin? Come sit by me my pretty one," Solange purred, patting the spot on the bed beside her. She could barely contain herself with the mortal's heartbeat pounding in her head.

Augustin pushed the whimpering mortal down on the bed as Solange got up on her knees. The woman began to cry harder as Solange pulled her close. Her pulse quickened under her lips as Solange kissed and licked her neck. The woman screamed as Solange latched on to her, sucking hard and fast as the women tried to fight. Augustin grabbed her arms and bit into the other side of her neck. The prostitute ceased struggling, her pulse weakening under their strong grasp. Sated and on fire, Solange and Augustin drank until he tossed the dead woman off the bed and climbed on top of his vampire lover.

Christian picked up Ross's scent just outside the precinct. He followed it around the west side of the reservoir, then north over the Great Hill to Block House No. 1, where it ended. Christian sniffed the air and leaped up onto the top of the structure. The smell of blood assailed his senses and he knew in his heart, even before he touched the sticky, wet snow on top of the dilapidated structure that it was Ross's blood.

He sniffed the air again and wondered where his body was hidden. The powerful vampire jumped off the roof and kicked in the rotten padlocked door that led to a small room underneath. The room was empty. He checked his watch. It was almost nine. As he headed back toward the museum, skirting the reservoir, he smelled something. He left the trees for the running track and noticed something on the ground up ahead—a wallet. He picked it up, and Ross's scent hit him again. Christian opened the wallet and counted one hundred dollars in loose bills. This had not been a robbery. Christian imagined Gaétan hoisting the detective's body over his shoulder like a sack of potatoes. The wallet must have fallen out of his pocket as he was carried away. But where had Gaétan disposed of him?

He smelled Amanda's scent before he rounded the corner; he was glad she was waiting for him. He wondered if she had any regrets about sleeping with him. The loss of his mortal friend seemed too much to bear at the moment and the vampire shoved his grief aside as he came around the museum toward Fifth Avenue. He prayed that Ross had not suffered for Christian's arrogance and stupidity.

How could I have expected him to face Gaétan alone? Am I losing my mind?

Chapter Twenty-five

❧

AMANDA CHECKED HER watch. It was just after nine o'clock. A warm front had brought an unusual amount of joggers and walkers to the park, more the usual for a Friday night this time of year. She had forsaken her hat and gloves and was enjoying the warm weather, although she knew it would be short lived; after all, it was only early February. She climbed the steps to the main doors of the museum to get a better view of Fifth Avenue. She was eager to see Christian, but also nervous. She wondered about the terra cotta statue and made a mental note to ask him about it.

She knew now that Christian's presence in her life was more than coincidence. It was kismet, just as she had told Michel. As she reached into her purse for her cell phone, she noticed him at the bottom of the steps with his hands in his coat pockets. How long had he been standing there? She smiled, taking her time to walk back down the steps.

"Hello," he said with a smile, his voice making her knees shake. You came . . . I wasn't sure ..."

Amanda felt herself blush as she remembered the previous night. "Did you get my note?"

He nodded and she instinctively placed her hand through his arm as they walked toward the park. They had not gone very far when she brought up the news story about the missing detective. His dark eyes caught hers assuring her that Ross had nothing to do with the crime. Just when she felt ready to ask him about the statue in his library, he changed direction.

"Where are you taking me?" She asked, stopping in her tracks.

"It's one of my favorite places in the world." He smiled, cupped her face in his hands and kissed her. She kissed him back more passionately.

"Will you come home with me again tonight?" He whispered, taking her hand again.

She smiled up at him. "It was never a question."

They approached Bethesda Terrace in silence, stopping at the stone railing that overlooked the fountain. Christian held her in his arms in front of him.

He tried to block from his mind the fact that Gaétan was her special friend Thomas. The man on the phone; the same man who had thanked her for their night spent together. Amanda had been seduced by him, and the last thing Christian wanted was for her to confront the ancient vampire. He knew she would, and it would only get her killed, or much worse. It was time to tell her the truth. He began talking into her hair; it smelled of his own shampoo.

"Your brother was executed because he possessed something very threatening to the vampires that attacked you both in the park. Actually, they came here to kill you both that night, but fortunately I was able to stop them."

He felt her tense up at the memory of it.

"What is it they want from me?"

Christian thought it best to just say it without beating around the bush. "You and Ryan are the descendants of a mortal woman and a vampire. They want your blood, Amanda. It is very powerful."

She turned to face him. "Holy shit, you're telling me I am the descendant of a vampire?"

Christian ran his hand through his hair. "The blood you possess gives us the power to walk in the daylight."

She began to back away. He knew it was too much to comprehend, and he worried that he would lose her.

He approached her slowly. "Amanda, listen to me. For some of us this would be considered a great gift, to walk freely in the daylight."

"But these vampires don't believe that, do they? That's why they killed Ryan."

"To them you are a threat to the natural order of things; an abomination that must be destroyed. I have watched over all of you mortals and after I discovered your unique gifts, I have been trying to protect you without involving you. After you saw me in the park, I figured I could erase your mind and you would have no memory of any of it. Unfortunately, it was more difficult that I had originally anticipated. I could not erase your thoughts."

"Do you see me that way, as an abomination, a freak?"

"I can't believe you have to ask me that, Amanda. Of course not, but they are afraid that I will take your blood for myself which would make me strong enough to return to Paris and overthrow them. They don't understand that I don't want that kind of power."

As he explained their thinking to her, he felt like a hypocrite, and he hated hypocrisy more than almost anything else. Perhaps she had no idea what he had done to her in the heat of passion.

"What was it like, tasting my blood? Am I really different?"

"Amanda, I . . ." He ran a hand through his hair, at a loss for words. "I—"

"Maybe it was for the best that it happened last night. Maybe you won't ever be tempted again, but it was the most erotic experience I have ever had."

He pulled her closer. "I promise you it will never happen again."

"How did they find out about us?"

"Ryan was donating his blood for money, and though I tried to prevent it, rumors quickly spread about the mortal with the unusual blood. Vampires are notorious gossips. Solange sent Lucien here to kill him, and he found out about you as well. He escaped me that night, but not before taking a supply of your brother's blood with him back to Paris."

"Who is Solange?"

Christian pulled back, taking her hand again. They walked in silence up the ornately carved stone steps of the terrace and headed south down Poets Walk. The snow-covered trees formed a white canopy over them. He had to tell her the truth.

"Solange is the child I had with Josette," he explained, unable to meet her stare.

"The union between a vampire and a mortal. Up until a few days ago, I believed she was my daughter. I whisked her to safety when she was a little girl, and sent her to be raised by a French family leaving Paris for London. Although I always kept my distance, I still watched over her as she grew up. Then she married and had a child of her own."

Christian was unsure of how much to tell her. He listened to her footsteps as they walked; they created a somber rhythm in the snow.

"Then in 1814, Yellow Fever raged through London. I heard a rumor that Solange was very sick. I refused to see her or do anything to save her life. Later.....she was turned and —"

"You left her to die?"

Christian stopped and met her gaze.

"Remember what I told you the other night, that you can have anything from me but immortality? You don't want this," he stammered as he fought to keep control of his emotions. "I would never give this to anyone, despite my love for them."

Amanda heard the sorrow in his voice. She reached up and touched his cold cheek. "Forgive me. I wasn't judging you. It would be an impossible decision for any parent."

He stared down at her in silence fighting his urge to cry for so many things, the most recent being Ross's death. He looked past her, ashamed of his actions; he needed her, yet feared his own longings.

"I thought I was doing the right thing, but I abandoned her and she hates me. I can never change that."

"Well now that you know the truth perhaps you can tell her yourself and mend things between you both."

He ran his hands through his hair. "It's not that simple, Amanda. A vampire named Gaétan turned her to spite me. They returned to Paris as lovers, where they ruled until he came here last fall to finish what Antoine could not. He fueled her hatred of me and hate is a great motivator."

"So is love, Christian. Perhaps it's not too late for you both, despite this Gaétan fellow."

"That fellow is here to slaughter you, Amanda."

"He's here now?" She glanced around her in the darkness. "He's here to kill me?"

Christian tried to comfort her, but it was no use. She began shivering in fear. He led her back up East Park Drive toward his home.

"So why did he want to spite you?"

"I stole Josette, the woman in the painting, away from him. They had been lovers when I was the lover of one of the most powerful vampires in Paris—Gabrielle. She sired me and Michel, and she became very jealous of Josette. Gaétan was already angry with me for stealing Josette, and in their bitterness and anger they formed an alliance against us."

He stopped again; Amanda's mouth was hanging open. "It's history, but unfortunately, it isn't ancient, my love." He gently closed her mouth, wishing he felt as cavalier as he tried to come across to her.

"So who fathered Solange if you didn't?" Amanda finally asked as Christian hit the security keypad and opened his front door.

A cold energy brushed up against them, like opening the freezer door on a hot summer day. Michel came out of the library and shut the door behind him.

"We have to talk, mon ami." Michel stood outside the library doors.

Christian ran his hand through his thick hair. "What is it, Michel?"

"You are not going to believe who's here."

Christian realized he had no idea what Michel meant by it.

"Is Solange in New York? Have you seen her?" He rushed to the window just as Michel uttered her name.

"Gabrielle is here."

Christian stopped as if he had hit a brick wall, not sure whether he had heard his best friend correctly.

"Gabrielle?"

"She's here, Christian. She's in the library and she's scared to death."

Chapter Twenty-Six

"SHE'S WHAT?" CHRISTIAN was still not sure if he had heard Michel correctly. "She's here? Is she alone?"

Michel grabbed him by the shoulders. "She came to the club tonight seeking asylum. All hell has broken loose in Paris."

For Christian, Gabrielle's presence solidified his worst fears. Letting out the breath he had not realized he was holding, he barged through the French doors with Amanda and Michel close behind. He tried to imagine her after all these centuries. Rationally, he knew she would look the same; vampires never aged, but how had she weathered the passing of time? He wondered if she still had that haughty façade coupled with exotic good looks. She had been his lover, his maker, and his enemy yet as he approached her, he could not discern which role he would see her in now.

She stood near the fireplace with the light behind her. It had been nearly three hundred years since he had seen the woman he had once loved, the woman who had turned him after taking his best friend away. Sadness, loss, and rage clouded his perception, and though her face had not changed, something about her seemed less confident and sure of herself. She was dressed entirely in black, with a mid-calf leather coat, silk pants, and high-heeled pumps. It was odd seeing her in contemporary clothing. Low-cut flowing gowns and black corsets suited her best.

As he slowly approached, he tried to comprehend the reality of her standing in his home. He was sure that the why of it would be equally devastating, but for the moment her presence rendered him speechless. He noticed Amanda out of the corner of his eye watching the two of them as if a spotlight shone down on them alone. He managed to keep his confusion off his face. Michel seemed happy to see her, or at least less guarded. Then there was Gabrielle. Was she happy to see him or still angry with him for loving Josette?

Her seductive voice broke the silence as he approached her. "It's been a long time, Christian."

He gracefully knelt down in front of her and bowed his head. She turned his face toward her, kissed him then nicked his lip, drawing blood. Christian slowly stood up; at his full height towering over her.

"Let me look at you." She smiled, her fangs bared. He stepped back, having fulfilled what protocol demanded of him. He thought her dark eyes were still seductive, but cold and bottomless, just like her nature. Her once long wavy hair now fell to her shoulders in a stylish cut, and tiny diamond earrings glistened in each ear. He thought he had remembered her beauty, but his mind's eye had distilled just how exotic and stunning she was, and despite the tumultuous history between them, Christian found her to still be one of the most beautiful women he had ever known or bedded.

"You both must be wondering why I am here." She turned her dark gaze toward Michel as if she had just noticed him. He had taken a seat on the couch, and was half hidden in the shadows.

"Since you came here sans invitation, this is either a declaration of war or you need our help. I am betting on the latter." Christian snapped, taking charge of his emotions again.

She forced a smile and Christian thought she looked like a cobra, poised and calm, yet able to strike on a moment's notice.

"These are dark times, gentlemen. I assume Gaétan has not fulfilled his mission since she still has her head, but the question is why."

Christian gestured for Amanda to come forward. *Like Dorothy meeting the wizard.* Christian watched Gabrielle drink in the frightened mortal.

"You're the one who all the fuss is about, aren't you?" Her gaze went from Amanda's head down to her shoes.

"And you must be Gabrielle, the lucky woman who made these gentlemen what they are today."

No one moved. Gabrielle folded her arms across her chest and chuckled.

"This is true." She smiled, and the air suddenly felt more breathable.

"Why are you here Gabrielle?" Michel asked still seated.

"I came here because there is no more alliance. Gaétan has not kept his end of the bargain—"

"Which was?" Christian interrupted her.

She pointed at Amanda. "To bring back her head and thwart the possible return of you both."

"Don't tell me you still believe his paranoid fantasies, Gabrielle? I realize he served a purpose when I left you, but you can't honestly tell me—"

She spoke through clenched teeth. "He killed Lucien and took the blood he stole from the mortal boy. We knew that but we could not prove it. Solange is too stupid to think beyond the latest fashions and her next conquest, so she never questioned her lover, but somehow she always manages to get them to do her dirty work."

Her description of Solange reminded Christian of his best friend, and the nagging thought crossed his mind again. *Could he have fathered her?* He watched Michel watching Gabrielle. There seemed to be little animosity between them, and he wondered if he still cared about her. Christian gestured toward the couch.

She seemed to flow, not walk, to the couch where she sat down. Michel sat to her right, and Amanda sat closest to the fireplace where Christian stood.

"Where is Étienne, Gabrielle? Why isn't he with you?"

She looked at each of them before speaking, her attention always riveted on Christian.

"Yes, is the old boy afraid to leave our beloved city?" Michel joked, smiling at her.

"I'm afraid Étienne is dead."

"What?" Both vampires shrieked.

"He's dead," she repeated, her voice suddenly flat. "He was murdered."

Christian tried to steady himself against the mantle. "Étienne murdered?"

"Oh dear God, what happened?" Michel asked staring at Christian.

The sound of the crackling fire wood cut the silence.

"Who is he?" Amanda interrupted panicked by the pain she saw in all their faces.

"He was a mortal boy who we stumbled upon in the Bois one night. He was begging for money and food," Michel began, and then stopped. Christian picked up the tale and explained to Amanda his role as their human servant until Gabrielle turned him. Gabrielle licked her lips nervously, and with great difficulty she explained how their love affair had ended and he had returned to the catacombs.

Gabrielle spoke about staying with some friends one night and coming home to find her luxurious apartment ransacked. Rumors began to surface that Étienne had been murdered, chained in the Bois, and she knew she had to leave Paris or die at the hands of Solange and her new lover, Augustin. She described Augustin's ruthlessness and reputation for being power-hungry. She slowly got up and handed something to Christian before he could protest.

"He would want you to have it."

Christian opened his hand to find a silver filigree signet ring, just like the one he, Michel, and Sabin wore every day. They had them made in Paris as a token of their allegiance to one another and a way of life that was quickly disintegrating in the chaos of the Revolution. He fought back tears.

"He gave it to me when things were good between us," she confessed, and Christian thought he heard her voice crack. Christian felt his stomach twist into a knot as he imagined Étienne burning up in a slow, painful death.

Suddenly Gabrielle was at the fireplace, standing close to Christian. "I need to speak to you alone."

Christian's eyes grew dark as the air shifted in the small room.

"This is not the Gaspard's drawing room, and I am no longer beholden to you. Anything you have to say, you say in front of both of them."

She touched his face, running her fingers over his fine features as if she were blind, yet trying to memorize them. Christian knew the games she had always played with him. She slipped her hand beneath his coat, and he felt her cold hand against his chest. Then she slid her hand lower, lingering near his groin.

"Come back home with me, Christian. We can crush her together. It can be like it once was between us—"

"Gabrielle, please!" He interrupted, stepping away from her. "New York has been our home since 1901. We stay here, remember. It was his life for our freedom, or have you forgotten our bargain?"

"Christ, won't you forgive and forget?" Standing up on her tiptoes, she kissed him passionately. He fought not to respond to her. "We can be like we once were back in Paris." She clung to him. "Don't you remember what it was like for the three of us then?"

It took every ounce of his self-control not to answer her.

"Gabrielle." He spit out her name as if it were poison on his lips. "There would not be enough time for me to adequately explain the reasons. Is that why you came here, to try to seduce me with delusions of power and bloodshed? Haven't you had enough of both?"

"I offered you the throne, and you turned me down." She ran a hand through his thick hair. "You were always too introspective and pragmatic, even as a young man." She rubbed up against him. Then she took his hand and ran it over her round backside. Christian let her play her games. The quicker she tested him, the faster she would tire of him and leave them alone. It was always the same dance between them. She tried to seduce him, and he fought her with his silence.

"Why did you turn against us?" She asked, caressing his stomach and then sliding her hand lower, toward his groin. Christian stepped back.

"I never turned against you, Gabrielle. I just did not agree with your politics. Have you forgotten how many young ones you seduced and then destroyed?"

Her expression did not change, yet Christian knew she was furious with him. After all these centuries, she had never lost her passion for him. Hiding his emotions had kept him safe from her. Emotion was like blood for Gabrielle. The more you spilled, the more she wanted, until your deepest feelings, fears, and needs filled her up, fueling her.

"Michel, talk some sense into him."

Michel stepped in to defend his best friend. "Those days are long over Gabrielle. If you want to stay alive, which I believe you do, then these games must end. We are trying to save Amanda's life."

Christian felt his anger growing as Gabrielle came towards Amanda. He watched her try not to show her fear as she stood up to face the all-powerful vampire.

Christian put himself between the two women. "Don't even think about it, Gabrielle."

"Smitten with another mortal, are you? You never learn Christian. Gaétan was right. You want her blood for yourself, don't you? Étienne and I defended you—"

The slap echoed around the room. Gabrielle barely flinched as Christian pulled the machete from his back.

"Christian, no!" Amanda screamed. "Enough of this fighting. This won't solve anything."

The vampire looked into the eyes of the young woman he loved more that life itself, and saw the fear and compassion she felt for a woman that would kill her without another thought. Her humanity moved him as he slowly put the machete back in its sheath.

Christian watched Gabrielle try to regain her composure.

"You can thank her now for saving your pathetic life. Don't you ever accuse me of being a bloodthirsty whore like you, Gabrielle."

Gabrielle tried to smile at Amanda though Christian knew she was rattled, yet it was impossible. Gabrielle hated mortals. It was as if she had no memory of being one.

He motioned for her to sit down. "Nothing has changed, Gabrielle, yet you said the alliance is dead. We know Gaétan is here, but he has not had a chance to strike."

Christian reached into his coat pocket and tossed something to Michel, who opened it up. Amanda could not see what it was right away.

"I found it in the park tonight near the reservoir. It belongs to Ross," he explained, speaking to Michel. "I also found his blood on the roof of Block House No. 1."

"Blood?" Amanda chimed in as all three vampires turned toward her. "His disappearance has been all over the news, and he's a suspect in the robbery at the museum. Now you're telling me he's been hurt?"

"He stole the sculpture, Amanda, in order to flush him out," Michel pointed at Christian.

She met Christian's gaze. "Amanda, Ross is dead—"

"Who are you talking about that you need to flush out?"

It was Christian who spoke up. "We all know him as Gaétan, but you know him as Thomas, the night guard at the museum."

"I don't understand….what? He's my friend. How the hell do you know who he is, Christian?"

"Come and sit down before you pass out." Gabrielle gestured to her.

Christian tried to couch an explanation in kindness. "Amanda, he's been here since the fall. Working in the museum and becoming your friend is a part of the ruse. He came here to kill you, but the fact that you are still alive means he has decided to keep you for himself."

"He's been here in New York since August when he told us he would bring your head back as proof he had killed you." Gabrielle said matter-of-factly. "Since you are still alive it leads me to believe he has other plans for you."

"But . . . but he's been with me during the day . . . he sometimes works day shifts. Has he been drinking my brother's blood?"

Gabrielle nodded and looked at Christian. "Yes, but he must be running out by now."

"I can't believe it. There has to be some kind of mistake here."

"There is no mistake, Amanda." Michel shrugged. "He's a very powerful vampire, and he will kill you if we don't get to him first. He has been surviving on killing innocent homeless people in Central Park. Ross was investigating it."

"He's been there for me, helping me with my research, buying me cups of coffee, and hanging out with me late at night when I had deadlines to fulfill. Look, it's just coincidental."

"What is it you do?" Gabrielle asked hesitantly.

Despite her audience, she took the opportunity to talk about her love of art and her passion for history and museums. Gabrielle and Christian listened intently, especially when she spoke of her love of eighteenth-century France. Michel seemed utterly bored and stared off into the fireplace as if he were a million miles away.

Chapter Twenty-Seven

AMANDA LOOKED AT her watch. It was three o'clock in the morning. She was growing tired and hoped she could curl up in Christian's bed. Michel arranged for a cab to take Gabrielle back down to the Grey Wolf; she would be staying in the bedroom behind their office. After saying their good-byes, Amanda found herself alone in front of the fireplace trying to digest the events of the evening.

She was tired, but she knew she would never fall asleep. Had Christian been spying on her? Is that how he had known her friend's name? Maybe there had been a mistake. None of it made sense, and she suddenly felt so alone.

"Why don't you come upstairs and get some sleep," he whispered, massaging her shoulders.

She was having a hard time reconciling that Thomas was a murderous vampire. In fact, all of it seemed absolutely crazy. Maybe the thing to do was go home and crawl into her bed and try and get some sleep. She spotted her coat on the couch and went for it.

"Where are you going at this hour, Amanda?" Christian asked as she her put on her coat and picked up her purse.

"I need to make sense out of what you are telling me. It's almost impossible to believe."

"You saw what happened to Ryan, how could you be so . . . dismissive, Amanda?" Christian stood casually at the door to the library.

"Not only did I see what happened to him, but I will never forget it, Christian. It's just too much to think about right now. How do I know that you aren't just jealous of my friend and making this up? You seem to know everything about me . . . Maybe you're just a crazy stalker who wants me dead . . . maybe . . ."

He tried to take her in his arms, but she pulled away.

"I want to go home to my familiar, boring apartment and my best friend. Please let me go."

"Fine, don't let me stop you," he sneered and opened the French doors. "Let Tony call you a cab."

"No, I need to walk," Amanda snapped back, almost running into Tony in the foyer. He seemed confused and frightened by what was happening, and she could not blame him. She felt the same way. Amanda opened the front door and the cold night air hit her. Tears streamed down her face, blurring her vision as she ran down the steps onto the sidewalk. There was no one on the dark quiet street as she headed toward Fifth Avenue and the museum. After walking half a block, she realized her stupidity.

What was I thinking? How can I get a cab up here at three in the morning?

Her only other alternative was to take the subway, which suddenly seemed appealing in its familiarity. *I need normal right now. This is all too crazy, like a bad dream.* She was almost at the corner when a figure emerged from the shadow of a high rise. *Great, now I'll get raped. That will just top off the evening.* Not sure which way the stranger was walking, she stopped, thinking he might cross Fifth Avenue, heading uptown.

"Amanda?" He called out in the darkness. His voice sounded strangely familiar.

Then he stepped into the streetlight wearing a long black coat like Christian's and high-heeled boots. His hair was tied back, but his face was unmistakable. He smiled and there was no doubt in her mind.

"Thomas, is that you?"

"The one and only."

He approached her with a smile frozen on his handsome face, and a million thoughts ran through her head, the most important one being, what was he doing here? Was this pure coincidence, which she did not believe in, or was he following her? His footsteps made no sound on the frozen ice and snow, just like Christian's.

"What are you doing here?" Amanda thought about dialing 911, but her cell phone was in her purse, zipped up and secured over her shoulder. There was no way she would reach it in time.

As he came closer his face changed and the smile was gone.

"I have a score to settle with an old friend, with whom it seems you have managed to fall hopelessly in love, which is unfortunate for you both."

She could not believe what he was saying. "I haven't heard from you in days. You could at least have had the decency to call me and quite frankly, who I'm seeing is none of your business."

He glanced up at Christian's townhouse. "Oh, but it is my business, Amanda. You're my business, and now it's time to come with me."

She backed away from him. "Who the hell are you?"

"How rude of me not to introduce myself." He smiled as he came closer. "My name is Gaétan."

Gaétan fought not to listen to her ranting or to feel sorry for her. They had become close friends, despite his hatred of Christian. He had enjoyed their late night talks in her office. Whether it was work related or the latest movie she had seen over the weekend, they had fun together. She spoke of art and history with such passion and enthusiasm, her face so serious and her eyes so dark and intense. He had played at being a mortal man, and though he hated to admit it, he had enjoyed being with her. *But it's her blood I need to survive.*

He barely remembered being mortal, but as he thought back over his endless existence, he found that Amanda was a bright spot, just as Josette had been centuries ago. He wished he could tell her about his life and about living through the Revolution. She would have appreciated his struggles, his loyalty to the throne of France. In quieter moments, he thought of abandoning his plan and returning to Paris and Solange and leaving Christian to his own life here in the new world.

In saner moments, he had thought he could remain Thomas, the night guard at the Met, and work with her. Then his rage consumed him; his revenge fed him like the blood he needed from her to walk in the sunlight. Ah, the sunlight. He had become addicted to the freedom and power it gave him, but he had run out of Ryan's blood days ago. He had to strike now.

I cannot let Christian have her.

"Gaétan," she said. "You don't have to do this, please just let us be."

He could hear her heart racing in his ears, and the musky smell of her fear aroused him.

"You have become very dear to someone I abhor. I will not allow him to have you, ever." He found himself lost in her beautiful eyes.

"Then you have me," she whispered. "Take me home again."

"I'll kill him and have you, my dear. No need to worry about that."

Amanda stepped back and she caught her foot on the ice, almost losing her balance. He came toward her and as she turned to run she slammed into something solid as arms grabbed her. Before she could scream, Tony was there. Christian came out of the shadows, machete in hand. Gaétan hissed and pulled a sword out of his coat.

"So, we finally meet again, Christian."

Christian snickered at his old enemy. "Give it up, Gaétan. Go home while you still have your head."

"Do you know how long I have waited to face you in combat again?"

"It's over, Gaétan. The alliance is dead."

Gaétan dropped his guard for a moment, unsure of himself.

"That's right. Gabrielle is here seeking asylum and those were her exact words. Étienne is dead at the hands of your lover and Augustin. You are a dead man if you set foot in Paris, and you are most certainly are a dead man if you stay here."

"You liar!" Gaétan hissed, and rushed Christian.

"Take her back to the townhouse now," Christian commanded Tony, dodging his sword.

"No!" Amanda screamed as Tony dragged her away.

"If I don't come back, get her out of here as fast as possible."

"Let me go," she screamed and broke free of Tonys' embrace.

Amanda felt her jacket rip off as she tried to get to Christian.

"Amanda, come back here," Tony yelled, racing after her as she ran back up the street.

"Where are they, god damn it?" She cried on the verge of hysteria. "I have to find him, Tony."

He grabbed her again and stared into her wild eyes. "Listen to me, Amanda. He's lived for centuries. Christian can take care of himself."

"You don't understand. The sun's coming up. Thomas can stand it but Christian can't survive. He'll die out there."

Her body went limp, and Tony led her back to the townhouse. She sobbed into his sweatshirt and muttered how much Christian was the love of her life. Tony set her down on the couch and then reset the alarm on the front door. He stoked the fire while Amanda sat in a daze, trying to piece together the facts that Ross was dead and her friend Thomas really was a monster after all.

"How could I have been fooled by him, Tony?" She asked. She hadn't felt this vulnerable since her brother had been murdered last summer. "I slept with him, Jesus Christ." She ran her hand through her hair, exhausted yet unsure how she could ever sleep again.

Tony knelt in front of the fireplace and turned to face Amanda, his amber eyes aglow from the fireplace light.

"We're all blinded by love, Amanda. It sucks, but that's just the way it is."

She sat transfixed by the fire while Tony fixed her a sandwich and some tea. He set the tray of food down on the coffee table and then sat beside her.

The peppermint tea felt good on her throat. She took a few bites of the sandwich and put it down. She felt sick to her stomach.

"It's good, but I can't eat right now. What do we do now?"

Amanda hated feeling inert, and being this powerless was driving her crazy. She turned away from Tony, embarrassed by her tears.

"We wait," he said with a shrug. "There's not much else we can do. He's a very powerful vampire, Amanda. He'll be fine."

Amanda wondered how that could be true. The sun was coming up soon, and Christian could not survive it. She could not fathom that these beings from a world she never thought existed were hunting her, trying to kill her just for being alive, or that she was a descendant of a woman named Solange. Who was the vampire who had really fathered Solange?

Maybe if I can get to her, I can explain everything and she won't want to kill my Christian.

Tony pushed the sandwich plate toward her. "Try to eat, Amanda."

She took a bite and tried to swallow, but it just sat in her throat like lead. She washed it down with some tea.

"So, how did you end up with Christian and Michel, if I may ask?"

"I used to hang out at the Grey Wolf and . . . I was a donor, sometimes... I just accepted them for what they are."

"What's a donor?" Amanda asked, setting down her mug and remembering Ryan's exact words. *I give blood and I get paid.*

He smiled as if remembering something prurient. "It's real simple. A donor gives blood for sex or money, depending on the situation."

"My brother was hanging out there, too. Maybe you knew him? Ryan Perretti?"

Tony shrugged. "There were always a lot of people hanging out there, Amanda."

"He and I looked a lot alike . . . He had a drug problem. He told me he was giving blood for money."

"There was this one kid, dark-haired like you. Christian took a real interest in him. I thought he was taking his blood, but Christian's . . . he's different. He has an interesting view of right and wrong, and he seemed to be protecting this kid. Then the kid left I guess. I didn't see him around anymore. When he tried to convince me to leave the club, I told him I had no money and nowhere to go so he offered me this job."

Amanda smiled. She wondered if Tony had been a junkie as well. "Sounds like it worked out for you, and you both really respect each other."

"Yeah, well, they're vampires, you know? I mean, you just don't fuck with 'em. "

Amanda forced another bite of her sandwich while Tony stood by the fireplace smoking a cigarette. She knew he was nervous as well, despite his protests.

If only Christian had offered Ryan a job, maybe he would be alive today.

"Christian asked you to get me away from here if he doesn't come back. What did he mean by that?"

Tony took a long drag from his cigarette.

"He wants you put on a plane to San Francisco."

"Why San Francisco?" she asked, putting her mug of tea down on the coffee table.

"He lived there when he and Michel left London. He mentioned a woman's name. He followed her there in the late eighteen-hundreds. Monique something. She's long dead but there is a vampire living there that he trusts."

Amanda felt her breath catch in her throat. "Monique Moulin?"

"Yeah, something like that. She lived in San Francisco and then got married and came to New York."

Could Christian have known her great-great-great-great-grandmother? She had lived in California and moved to New York when she married Charles Devereaux. Is that when Christian had come here, too? It all made sense in such a crazy way. She took her shoes off and put her head back on the couch, mumbling to Tony that she just needed to rest for a moment. She made him promise to wake her when the sun rose.

Chapter Twenty-Eight

❧

CHRISTIAN FOLLOWED HIS enemy farther into Central Park, knowing that each step led him closer to his possible demise. There wasn't much time until sunrise, yet rage pushed him farther north into the more remote area of the park. Just when he thought he had lost him, he noticed Gaétan silhouetted against the lightening sky atop Block House No. 1. It took all his willpower not to charge him.

"So have you figured out who sired the child?" Gaétan called out in his familiar raspy voice.

Christian said nothing yet he clenched the hilt of his machete tighter.

"She cuckolded you right in front of your eyes," he laughed, enraging Christian. "What kind of a man allows his best friend to share his woman?"

"What kind of a man seduces his daughter," Christian snapped back while Gaétan laughed.

"You know I did not sire Solange." He smiled, "even as a child you could not help but see the resemblance to Monsieur Baptiste. He seduced Josette right under your nose."

Before he could think, he was on the roof with Gaétan, their weapons dancing in the predawn light. They cut each other, but their wounds healed instantly as they jumped and swirled around each other like a tornado. Despite his speed and strength, his enemy was older and stronger, having survived on Ryan's blood for months.

"You were the laughing stock of the court, Christian. So devoted to that slut who—"

Christian tried to strike despite the slowly rising sun. There was no more time to fight. He had to seek shelter away from Gaétan before he burned to death. He jumped off the roof seeking shelter inside from the crisp winter sun. There was nowhere else to go; he was trapped and exhausted, and soon he would fall asleep, never to wake again.

He threw his long coat over his body and he curled up in a corner, waiting with his machete in hand. He knew he had only seconds until Gaétan stormed in to finish him off.

At least Amanda and I had one night together . . . Michel will be fine. Images, smells, and memories swirled inside of him, as the last few hundred years seemed to flash by in seconds.

It's never enough time, no matter how long you live.

The first rays of muted sun hit the window pane and crept silently across the dirt floor toward him like an assassin. Christian tried to steady his breathing and stay calm as he huddled closer in the corner. He waited for the pull of the darkness to take him.

The sun felt brighter now; it lit up a wider swath on the dirt floor, giving him only inches in which to hide. He had failed her and himself.

How could I have been so blind not to strike sooner? I love you, Amanda.

He thought of her beautiful face, her laughter, and the way she had looked at him. It was bittersweet, and now it was over as he felt his enemy approach along with the sun.

Christian had garnered all his strength as Gaétan entered the room. He felt his enemy behind him and Christian hoped Gaétan assumed he was asleep. He felt the sun on his boots, anticipating flames, but there was nothing. *It must be the blood.*

Suddenly he felt the blade cut through the air as Gaétan struck and with every ounce of strength he had left, Christian turned over and lunged before Gaétan could bring his sword down. Christian braced his body against the wall as screams filled the room. Christian sliced through the vampire's neck, severing his head in mid scream. As Gaétan's limp body fell onto the dirt floor he ignited. Christian tried to creep back into the corner as his enemy burned. Tears of joy streaked his dirty cheeks as he rolled over into the shadows and pulled his coat over his head. The smell of burning flesh, dirt, and blood filled his senses as darkness finally claimed him.

It was early Saturday morning when Amanda arrived back at her apartment. The familiar smell of fresh coffee made her realize how much she missed Bethany and her simple life.

"Where the hell have you been?" Bethany stepped out of the kitchen in her bathrobe holding a mug of coffee. "Are you all right?"

"I need a cup of coffee." She tossed her ripped coat onto the living room couch on her way to the kitchen. "I feel like absolute crap."

Bethany watched with her mouth hanging open while Amanda poured a cup of coffee.

Amanda searched the refrigerator for milk or cream. Finding a container, she opened it and took a sniff just to make sure it was still fresh. She judged it marginal and poured some into her cup. It was only after taking a long sip that she noticed Bethany staring at her.

"Amanda we need to talk."

Bethany pulled out a chair for herself and sat down across from her best friend. It was noon when Amanda finished telling her what had transpired since meeting up with Christian in Ross's office. Bethany had moved only once, to pour them both warmers. When Amanda finished, she felt cleansed and free of what had been such a bizarre secret. She tried to read Beth's face. Their friendship had survived a lot, but she would not blame her if she thought she was crazy. At the moment, she wasn't sure herself.

Bethany reached over and touched her arm. "If it wasn't you telling me this, I would think you were totally crazy, but I know you, and I met all the players, except Gabrielle and Tony, and I would have to say they did seem a little different."

Amanda finished her second cup of coffee. She felt lost and unsure of what nightfall would bring. Now she had exposed her best friend to a world that she still wasn't sure she believed in herself and made Beth privy to a robbery and a murder.

Bethany convinced her to have breakfast and made her famous French toast with bacon while they talked. As they ate, Amanda began to feel like her old self again. After breakfast, she took a hot shower and tried to sleep. Bethany offered one of her sleeping pills, but Amanda hesitated until Bethany explained that she only took them toward the end of tax season, just to take the edge off. Amanda took one and laid down on her bed, setting her alarm for five o'clock. Bethany had to go to work but promised to check in later. Amanda felt the drug pull her under and wondered if Christian had made it till dawn.

Something tickled his face. Something warm with a frenetic pulse. Christian opened his eyes in the darkness and grabbed at the rat sniffing his face. The creature squealed as he drained it. When he finished, he tossed it against the wall with a thud. His watch face glowed in the darkness; seven o'clock. Christian sat up; he felt weak from lack of blood. Then he remembered the battle and Gaétan's death. If he could get home, Tony or Michel would feed him. But he could barely stand up. It seemed to take forever to put his machete back in its sheath.

As he crawled towards the rotted doors, he sensed vampires hovering in the darkness. As hunger blinded him he pushed his way out into the darkness.

"Oh my god." Michel pulled his best friend up from the ground and brushed his matted hair away from his face. "You're alive."

"I'm so hungry." Christian whispered, clinging to his best friend.

In one fluid motion, Michel drew a tiny, silver dagger out of his black jacket. He sliced his chest and pulled Christian toward him. Christian put his arms around Michel and latched onto his chest.

When he no longer felt lightheaded, Christian forced himself to stop.

"What is it, Gabrielle?" Michel asked, buttoning his jacket up.

She shook her head as if shaking off sleep or a trance. "I never thought I would see the two of you again, let alone like this . . ."

Michel put his arm around Christian to steady him. Gabrielle tried to help but Christian refused her. As they walked through the park, Christian recounted what had happened to Gaétan. Michel suggested that a party was in order. As they approached the house, Christian noticed Tony in the window, a worried look on his young face. Christian knew the boy had nowhere else to go and had probably not slept all night.

Once safely at home, Tony rambled on about how he and Amanda had searched the park for him all morning, and then explained that she had gone home afterward. They had planned to rendezvous at dusk, but she had not called or shown up. Christian called her as he headed upstairs to the bathroom, but he got her voice mail and left a message. Tony ran ahead into the bathroom and turned on the bathwater, adjusting it to the temperature he knew Christian liked while dumping in some bath salts.

Christian tossed his cell phone on the bed and told Tony what had happened to Gaétan.

"So that means everything is okay now? Is Gabrielle staying here?"

"Would you like that, Tony?"

Tony shrugged as he stood watching the lean vampire slip out of his tattered shirt and dirty black jeans. He slid into the hot water and moaned in relief. He knew Tony was glad he was home safe.

Amanda woke with a jolt.

Oh shit, what time is it?

Rolling over she checked her cell phone. It was eight thirty. Her body hurt like she had a case of the flu, and her mouth tasted like cotton. She had several missed calls and four messages.

The first was from Bethany, who was calling to check in on her and hoped she was okay. She said she would come home if Amanda needed her to otherwise she was going to stay over at Jeff's place.

Anticipating the next message, she tried to sit up, as a wave of nausea hit her. Not sure if it was the pill or lack of sleep, she lay back down. The room began to spin. She closed her eyes as his voice filled her senses, soothing her and easing her pain. Was it supernatural power or love that made her feel like putty in his hands?

"Amanda, where are you? It's Christian. I'm alive and okay . . . Gaétan is dead. I'm going to get cleaned up. Call me please. I love you."

She replayed the message too many times to count.

The next two messages were from Christian, who was growing more and more panicked.

She decided to clean up before calling him back. Just as she had managed to get herself into the shower, she heard her doorbell ring.

Amanda grabbed her extravagant Christmas purchase off the door hook—a floor-length floral robe from her favorite department store. After quickly towel-drying her hair she ran barefoot to the front door.

"Just a minute." She peered through the eye hole. "Oh, my God," she cried, pushing and twisting the numerous locks on her apartment door. It crashed back against the wall as Christian stormed in.

Before she could respond, he had picked her up and was carrying her back into the bathroom. He slipped off his leather coat and let it fall to the floor. Unbuttoning his shirt, he pulled it over his head and tossed it to the floor as well. His white body was flawless, and his low cut jeans rested just right on his thin hips. He loosened the machete and set it down on the floor.

"All I could think about when faced with my death was losing you."

"What are you doing?" She asked as he reached in and turned on the shower.

"Taking a shower." He moved past her. "Will you be joining me?"

Chapter Twenty-Nine

❧

"IF I DIDN'T know you better, Michel, I would say that you are drunk."
Amanda laughed as he took her in his arms, dancing with her. She
and Christian had just arrived at the *Grey Wolf*, and Amanda could
feel the difference in the atmosphere. Even Sabin was smiling at the
news that Gaétan was dead.

"Stay close to Christian tonight." Michel whispered, pulling
her close.

She wasn't sure if she understood what he was saying, though
she sensed his unease.

"What are you so nervous about, Michel? Gaétan is dead." He
spun her around, smiling, though his eyes were serious.

"When the shit hits the fan, she will go after you. Christian will
try to stop her. Let me be the decoy."

At first Amanda had no idea what he was talking about and
then it hit her. He was speaking about Solange. She smiled up at
him sensing Christian was watching them. She pretended they were
speaking about nothing.

"What are you trying to say?" She asked, but she already knew in her heart.

"That I owe him more than I can ever repay." He twirled her again and pulled her close to him. "Christian is the noblest man I have ever known, living or dead. Do you understand me?"

Amanda nodded and wondered what it must have been like for him to father a child he could not raise with a woman he could never claim for himself. She wondered if Christian knew or at least suspected. But before she could ask he led her off the dance floor.

"You must be Amanda," Peter pressed his hand into hers.

Gabrielle and Eve eyed each other with a look between women that was universal, no matter the time or place. They were both dressed in beautiful, low-cut black dresses and were vying to be queen of the ball. Amanda found them both beautiful and elegant, and tried not to compare herself to them.

"Come, dance with me, pretty lady." Christian pressed his hand into hers and pulled her out onto the dance floor. Now that Gaétan was dead, they had their future ahead of them. In time she knew she could move beyond Detective Ross's death, the robbery at the museum, and Ryan's murder and finally get on with her life. She smiled up at him as he spun her around then pulled her close. The electronic club music was loud and discordant, but she felt calm and safe with him.

All was well, since Gaétan was dead. She would probably never be able to reconcile that monster with her friend Thomas, but in time, he would become just a memory, like the monsters that had murdered her brother. Amanda had never remembered crying so much over a man, but when Christian had come back to her unharmed her relief made her break down and sob.

They had just walked off the dance floor when her cell phone rang. She explained to Christian that it was Bethany and that she was going to call her back outside, rather than send a text message. There was just too much to tell her.

"What is it?" Amanda asked, noticing the look on his face.

"Nothing," he lied and forced a smile. "Make your call, but hurry back."

He watched her disappear into the crowd with a knot in his stomach. Though logically he knew that Gaétan was dead, what about Solange? When her lover didn't return to her, would she eventually come looking for him? Christian had always told himself he would kill her now, but he had not seen her since he had left London. Would he be able to maintain his steel resolve?

She's here already. I can feel her.

"You need to relax, my friend." Michel said with a wink and picked up a strand of Christian's hair. "How did your hair get all wet again?"

He tried to smile. "I don't kiss and tell, Michel."

Christian tried to read Michel's face. Did he seem antsy and on edge, or was Christian projecting his own fears onto his friend?

Did he father her?

"Michel," he whispered, suddenly feeling brave.

"So, I suppose you no longer need my services," Eve interrupted, speaking to Christian. She turned her back to Michel and tried to get Christian's undivided attention, but Michel cut in between them.

"You know, Eve, if I didn't hate you so much, I could really love you." He blew her a kiss.

Eve snarled back at the beautiful vampire before turning her attention to Peter, who was holding court with a couple of Goths at the other end of the bar.

"Boy is she barking up the wrong tree," Michel laughed, slipping behind the bar. His attention was drawn to a petite blonde with streaks of red and blue in her long hair. Christian studied the scene. He felt stronger and more focused since taking Amanda's blood again. He would give her just a few more minutes and then go looking for her. Bored, he began to flip through his received calls while he waited for Amanda to return. Ross's number came up and he hit send before remembering that Ross was dead.

Amanda had just hung up with Bethany when the couple brushed passed her. Something about their dress made her think they were foreigners. Amanda stepped aside to let them by, and suddenly she felt as if she were in danger. She tried to rush past them and back inside, but the man blocked her path.

"Amanda Perretti?" The woman spoke, with a thick British accent though her lips didn't seem to move. Amanda never would have mistaken her for Christian's or Gaétan's child. There was something about her jaw, the shape of her face and her high cheekbones and Amanda knew there was no mistaking it. She was Michel's child.

"Yes." She tried acting nonchalant, but she knew who they were and why they were in New York. She looked from the woman to the man who towered over her. He stared down at Amanda with bottomless eyes, and she knew they were both vampires.

The woman gestured at Amanda to walk away from the club toward the alley that ran the length of the building. They each came up beside her but said nothing. Before they had gotten too far, Amanda's cell phone rang.

Amanda reached into her pocket. "It's my . . . boyfriend . . . I'd better answer it."

The woman grabbed the phone right out of her hand. "Hello father, how are you? It has been such a long time."

"What is it you want Solange?"

"Your head on a stick..."

Solange snapped the phone closed and dropped it on the sidewalk then crushed it.

Amanda took a deep breath and tried to remain calm. Asking who they were and what they wanted was a waste of energy. She knew who they were and they realized that she was not surprised.

Grabbing Amanda by the arm, they continued down the alley. When they reached the end of the driveway, Augustin grabbed her around the waist and jumped. Before she could let out a scream, they had landed on the roof top of the club.

Solange pulled out her dagger and Amanda flashed back to last summer and her brother's murder. Solange slowly began circling her like a shark honing in on its prey. The wind began to pick up and Amanda wished she had her coat. Suddenly she came closer flashing her knife.

Solange snarled but Augustin stepped between them, pushing Solange away from the girl.

"Solange, this was not our plan."

"Look at her, she's . . . she's pathetic. I should drain her precious blood myself."

"No, Solange." He replied in a heavy French accent. Amanda tried to get a read on him. She guessed that they were lovers and that she had convinced him to come to New York with her to find Gaétan.

Solange snarled at Augustin as he pushed her back, and Amanda felt her sorrow and her rage.

"Where is Gaétan you little twit?"

"Gaétan is dead. He thought he controlled the blood, but it controlled him, an immortal obsession I suppose and it won out in the end."

Solange stormed past Augustin again with her dagger raised. Amanda tried to get away from her as Augustin turned to block the blow, but it was too late. Amanda heard herself scream as Solange sliced her arm through her blouse. At first she felt nothing, but as she glanced down at her arm and saw dark liquid oozing and dripping onto the ground she felt faint. Solange licked the dagger's blade as if she were kissing a lover, her lips caressing it and lapping up all traces of the mortal's blood.

Amanda hid behind Augustin. She knew he was the more rational one and might try to protect her, despite the fact that he was Solange's and would do anything she asked of him. They had come all the way from Paris for her and would stop at nothing. She felt a slight shift in the air and noticed Christian perched silently on a far roof top.

Chapter Thirty

❦

CHRISTIAN SNIFFED THE air, the scent of her blood filling up his senses. His skin crawled at seeing Solange lick her knife. A vampire he did not recognize guarded his beloved with a sword. It had been so long since he had seen Solange. He fought the feelings of hatred and guilt that rose up equally, blinding him. They were arguing over Amanda, speaking mainly in French. He knew that Amanda's blood was tantalizing to her as well. No vampire could resist it. Though he had tried to fight the pull, he could not resist her either. He had always thought himself a practical man, yet the fantasies of ruling the Parisian vampires had begun filling his head.

Be strong, Amanda. Do not show them you are afraid.

Augustin had forced Amanda to the ground and was holding his sword over her. If any of them tried to rescue her, he would kill her instantly. They were so focused on Amanda that they did not sense him as he slowly came toward them in the darkness, his machete sharp and glistening. He had ten minutes before Michel would also strike.

Is it the blood that keeps me hidden?

He focused on the sound of his leather coat flapping in the breeze and not on Amanda, pale and bleeding on the ground. The wound was deep, but she would live if that was all they did to her. Augustin argued for leaving now while they had Amanda, but Solange, fueled by both her hatred of her father and now Gaétan's death, wanted her revenge. They continued to argue as Christian came closer.

Something made her turn at the last moment, just as Christian was upon them.

Solange hissed and brandished her weapon at the man she called her father. "So, we finally meet again, Papa."

"This is between us, Solange. Let her go." His voice boomed in the darkness. Augustin raised his sword over Amanda.

Christian looked into the eyes of his daughter. He remembered what an elegant, kind woman she had been until she had been turned and poisoned by Gaétan, who had filled her head with lies about him. Some things were beyond repair. No matter how much time passed between them, it could not heal the deep chasm. Time had fed it, allowing their pain to grow and take shape into something ineffable and beyond grief. He had loved her so much, and had lived his life trying to protect her.

If Josette could see her now, she would be sick. What if she could see me now?

She laughed, and Christian felt his rage building. "You can't be serious, Father. She's the goose that laid the golden egg."

"I am not your father." Christian declared, staring into her empty eyes as she approached him.

"Why should I believe you?" She snarled, stopping just a few feet away from him and pointing back at Amanda. "So you can save her?"

"Josette led me to believe I had fathered you, and until recently I had no reason to doubt her. Now I am not sure what to believe."

She smiled, and he could see in her face how much she hated him.

There was no sense talking to Solange. Her hatred had given her life meaning, a focus in the murky timelessness of their existence.

"So, the mortal lied to you. Won't you ever learn not to trust them?"

"That was a risk I took Solange, and that mortal was your mother. She loved you dearly and paid for her patriotism with her life. I did as she asked and took you away to keep you safe."

For a second, the vampire's guard dropped, and then she snarled again and came closer.

"You always did like mortals more than your own kind."

"I must confess, Solange. It is my own kind that baffle me the most, and whom I have found myself unable to trust."

She began to circle him, and he felt her agitation. Augustin had picked Amanda up and pulled her close; the sword now lay across her neck. Christian glanced at Amanda and saw more than fear. She loved him and he knew it, just as he knew they might not survive the night.

"This mortal tells me Gaétan is dead. Is that true?"

Her dark eyes had become like black holes, deep and bottomless. She was struggling with her own rage, running the long flat blade of the dagger against her leg. Christian glanced at Amanda, who was shivering.

"He's dead, Solange. I destroyed him."

She was coming closer. He wanted to strike out at her.

"Let it end now, Solange. Take him and go home. Leave us in peace here."

"There is no peace between us." She stopped and twirled her hair with one hand as she contemplated his words.

"There can be. You have the choice. Your mother and Gaétan were lovers when I met her. She was the most beautiful woman I had ever known, and I see some of her in you. She loved you and only wanted you to live in peace. You were a mother before . . . You must remember what it is like to love a child."

"Oh, I do, but apparently you do not." She raised her dagger at him.

"No, please," Amanda shrieked. "It's me you want. Just take me and let him go."

"Amanda, you don't know what you're saying." Christian cried out.

"Oh, how romantic. She's trying to protect you." Solange stormed toward Amanda. "I will kill all of you."

"Solange, stop it." Augustin yelled at her. "There is time."

Just then Michel came over the rooftop brandishing a dagger and landed near them. "Come on you, bastard," Michel snarled at the young blond. "Don't hide behind the girl, come and get me."

Augustin pulled Amanda closer and raised the sword to her neck. Christian cringed at the sight of Amanda whimpering with the cold steel against her neck. "Drop the knife or she dies. Both of you drop your weapons." Augustin spoke as Christian nodded to his best friend.

Michel dropped the dagger and raised his arms in surrender, coming closer to them. Christian set his machete down on the ground.

"Stay away from her Michel." Christian yelled but Michel was already closer and even Christian could see the resemblance between the two of them. There was no doubt.

"If you are hell bent on killing someone then it's me you must vent your rage against, Solange. I am your father."

Christian froze as Michel kept talking.

'That's right, snarl at me, but it's the truth. I fathered you. I loved Josette and we….had an affair that lasted until her arrest in Paris. She knew I could never be devoted to either of you so she turned to him, the most loyal of us all."

Christian felt the knot in his stomach tighten as his best friend confessed.

"Why should I believe you?" Solange snapped at him.

"Because it's the truth Solange. Your mother loved you so much that she gave you up to save your life and Christian was the only person she trusted to get you to safety. So, now who do you want to kill?"

"Michel, you did not have to tell her anything," Christian shook his head in disgust.

"It was time my friend. I have kept this secret from you for centuries now and here she is to seek her revenge. I don't blame you a bit Solange; but go for the right vampire. Leave him alone."

Michel winked and smiled at his best friend. Christian had always wondered if he would ever be able to live without Michel. He could never imagine being separated from him and here they were on a roof top in New York City, the past not a blur to be remembered but a sorrow never addressed or set free. How had their entire lives together led to this moment?

Suddenly a fear Christian had long ago packed away like old love letters was now out in the open. So many years had passed between them with so much history, but it was only moments that now flashed through Christian's mind. So few poignant moments that made time suspend and the horror of this moment would last a lifetime for him as sorrow embraced him again. Christian felt like the scared boy in the stable again who just wanted to be with his best friend.

Amanda's screams echoed through the darkness as Augustin pushed her aside and lunged for Michel.

Christian ran to her just as Sabin and Gabrielle landed on the ledge and rushed Augustin. Augustin kept coming, but Sabin was too fast. Just as Augustin lunged at Michel, Sabin cut through him at the waist. His upper body careened off the ledge, while his legs crumbled, his sword clanging on the ground at his feet. He burst into flames as Solange ran towards him and grabbed his sword. Enraged, she came at Amanda, who had just gotten to her feet with Christian's help.

Amanda instinctively jumped in front of Christian, trying to protect him.

"No," Christian screamed as he pushed Amanda out of the way. She fell to the ground again.

He felt the blow as the sword pierced him and came through the other side.

Amanda heard the thud and screamed as he fell to the ground beside her.

He noticed how beautiful the night sky looked as pain radiated through him. He tried to grab the blade, but managed only to slice his fingers to shreds in an attempt to free himself. He heard Amanda yelling at the others to do something, and then Michel was there, stepping on Christian's chest to get leverage. He pulled at the hilt of the sword as it retracted through tissue and bone.

Gabrielle picked up his machete to chase Solange who was over the ledge in a flash, swallowed by the darkness. Gabrielle was back at Christian's side, tears flowing down her face.

"That bitch just missed his heart, but I think he might be dying." She wiped her tears.

"Christian," Michel cried, slapping his face.

Amanda crawled to his side and brushed his hair away, trailing blood across his pale face. She knelt closer to him, hoping he could hear her.

"You need blood. Take mine." She rolled up her sleeve. She shoved her arm in his face. "I don't . . . I don't know how much you'll need, but take it."

He wanted to tell her how much he loved her and that she had given his lonely existence meaning, but he could not make the words come. Through his blurred vision, he saw Sabin and Gabrielle standing over him, while Michel held him.

"No wait, lie down beside him." Michel directed. "Offer him your neck, Amanda."

She did as she was told and lay on the cold ground beside him. His body felt even colder as she pressed herself against him.

"Hurry before I lose my nerve."

Michel tore open her blouse.

She was shivering as she caressed him. "God damn it, Christian, do it."

He could hear her words echoing through his brain. He felt her pulse under his lips. If only he could move, bite into her neck, but it felt hopeless. He drifted into darkness farther away from them all.

"Just a small cut, Amanda." Michel whispered. She could feel the cold steel against her neck.

"Close your eyes, my dear." Gabrielle suggested; her face a kaleidoscope of sorrow and rage.

Closing her eyes, Amanda barely felt anything. She wasn't sure what had happened until she felt pressure as his cold lips latched onto her neck. As he bit into her, she felt her world spinning both in pain and pleasure. The sensation reminded her of the Tilt-a-Whirl at the local fair she had ridden with Bethany when they were kids. They had both laughed hysterically out of joy and fear as the ride careened out of control.

She felt someone holding her as she let go, and the sensation felt pleasurable and arousing as he drank her powerful blood. She was unable to focus on the words drifting through her head. It was as if she were in a dream.

"You will get cold as your body begins to shut down. Just try and hang on, Amanda. We won't let you die." Sabin spoke.

"You are the bravest person I have ever known, vampire or mortal." Michel whispered in her ear.

"Don't worry Amanda." A female spoke.

She was losing feeling in her hands and feet, and then she felt herself rising up into the darkness. She was hovering above them all, yet she was there lying on the ground while Christian fed from her, his hair spread out like a fan and she wondered if she would live through it.

She looked around her and noticed the two tiny flames that were all but extinguished. She rose higher over the rooftops on Bleeker Street, floating into the darkness of the night sky, past the stars, until she stood at the entrance of a tunnel filled with a white light. The warmth beckoned her as the light embraced her. She felt happy and safe again. Then she saw them emerge from a place beyond the light. She could feel their love, knowing her father and Ryan were waiting there for her. Amanda tried to move closer to them but something stopped her. She felt a pull as she fell back down into the night sky, past the stars. Then she recognized Bleeker Street and the rooftop of the Grey Wolf. She woke up to cold and darkness and the familiar faces of the vampires huddled around her.

Epilogue

UNUSUALLY TIRED, AMANDA took a break from packing to reread the article in the New York Times. It had made the front page, along with the discovery of Detective Ross's body in Central Park. Getting comfortable on the floral couch with the fireplace stoked up, Amanda slowly reread both articles, not sure which one she found more amazing.

A tall blond haired man had entered the museum at closing time and returned a terra cotta statue to the information desk. Though it was being tested for authenticity, it was believed to be the same statue that had been stolen from the museum just over a month ago. Witnesses said he was unfailingly polite. The NYPD was searching for him for further questioning.

Amanda shook her head. *Wait until he gets home.*

The adjacent article, along with a picture of Detective Burt Ross, explained the mysterious discovery of a body believed to be his found near the Reservoir. It appeared he was murdered, and that there was no connection between him and the robbery. Police were searching for one Thomas Bretagne, a security guard at the museum who disappeared the same night as Ross. Police asked anyone with information to please come forward.

Amanda glanced down at the small article, almost an afterthought, also on the front page. An afterhour's club in the West Village frequented by drug addicts and Goths had mysteriously burned to the ground in the early morning hours on Sunday. It was under investigation as well.

When worlds collide.

Amanda heard the front door open. Christian was home. She anticipated his silent footsteps as he came into the living room, wrapped in his usual black leather duster.

She set the newspaper down on her lap. "There is quite a lot of interesting reading today."

He shrugged and tossed the newspaper into the fireplace. They both watched it crumpled into flames.

He set his coat on a chair and sat down beside her. "You know what they say, believe half of what you read and none of what you hear."

He smiled and leaned over to kiss her.

As he stared into the eyes of the beautiful woman sitting beside him, the woman who had saved his life with her blood, he did not have the heart to tell her of his plan, his dreams. There was no one on the throne in Paris. Solange would have trouble holding her own without Gaétan or another strong male beside her. Perhaps they could make their peace and he could rule with Amanda beside him.

He wanted Michel as his second in command, though Michel had no interest in power. Sabin had already gone back to Paris to look for suitable lodgings for them all. Michel wondered if perhaps they could return to their childhood town of Meudon to live. So many plans and all in good time.

Time.

As he stared into Amanda's eyes he finally saw his future. He could hear two heartbeats now. She had no idea she was with child, nor did he have the heart to spoil the surprise for her.

She'll figure it out soon enough.

The irony of the situation was not lost on him. Was the child his or Gaétans? No matter, it was a miracle, just as Solange had been such a long, long time ago. It was as if his beloved Josette Delacore had returned from the grave to live on through his lovely Amanda. He would not lose her this time. He had learned his lesson well and as he stared into the fire, Christian tried not to look back, only ahead, since anything seemed possible.

Acknowledgements

THERE ARE MANY people who shared their encouragement and support while I was writing Immortal Obsession. You know who you are and I love you; however, I need to thank the following individuals for their unfailing guidance, humor and insight: Lou Aronica, The Fiction Studio; Linda Lauren, Sue Dolinko, Paul Murphy, Rita Vetere and the Anthro. Gang. To my reader, Debbie Vilage.

About Denise K. Rago

DENISE K. RAGO was born and raised in New Jersey, where she still resides with her family. Immortal Obsession is her first novel.

Visit www.DeniseKRago.com